Hansjörg Schneider, born in Aarau, Switzerland, in 1938, has worked as a teacher and journalist, and is one of the most performed playwrights in the German language. He is best known for his Inspector Hunkeler crime novels. *The Murder of Anton Livius*, following on from the success of *Silver Pebbles* and *The Basel Killings*, is the third in the series to appear in English. Schneider has received numerous awards, among them the prestigious Friedrich Glauser Prize for *The Basel Killings*. He lives and writes in Basel.

THE MURDER OF ANTON LIVIUS

Hansjörg Schneider

Translated by Astrid Freuler

BITTER LEMON PRESS
LONDON

BITTER LEMON PRESS

First published in the United Kingdom in 2023 by
Bitter Lemon Press, 47 Wilmington Square, London WC1X 0ET

www.bitterlemonpress.com

First published in German as *Hunkeler und der Fall
Livius* by Ammann Verlag, Zurich, 2007

The translation of this work was supported by the Swiss Arts Council Pro Helvetia

A CIP record for this book is available from the British Library

PB ISBN 978–1–913394–875
eB USC ISBN 978–1–913394–882
eB ROW ISBN 978-1-913394-899

Typeset by Tetragon, London
Printed and bound by CPI Group (UK) Ltd, Croydon CR0 4YY

swiss arts council
pr⊡helvetia

The author would like to thank Kriminalkommissär
Markus Melzl for reviewing the manuscript, and
contemporary witness Oskar Runser from Knoeringue,
Alsace, for information on historic events.

Peter Hunkeler, inspector with the Basel City criminal investigation department, formerly married with a daughter, now divorced, was asleep in his house in Alsace. He became aware that he was lying comfortably and that he was cosy and warm. He heard a faint purring. That was the black cat, he could feel it resting against the backs of his knees. He heard crowing. That was Fritz the cockerel in the henhouse. He heard a gentle snore. That was his girlfriend Hedwig, who was lying nestled against his belly. He opened his eyes and saw the cherry tree outside the window, its gnarled branches barely visible in the fog.

He remembered now: yesterday was New Year's Eve. They had danced at the restaurant in Zaessingue until three in the morning. Then they had meandered home along the side roads. They'd both had liberal amounts of red wine with their roast pork, and at midnight they'd popped the cork on a Crémant d'Alsace. The gendarmerie wasn't to be toyed with, even in the early hours of New Year's Day.

It had been a great night. The room was packed to the rafters, young and old all jumbled together. The band was from across the Rhine, from the Markgräflerland, with a young woman on accordion and a bald old fellow on drums, perhaps her father or her lover. They had all sung *Schützenliesl, bang bang bang, Happy New Year!* Even now, the music was still in his ears, the dance moves in his hips. He felt tired, light and happy. He shifted closer to Hedwig to drift back off to sleep.

But something cut through the quiet. A ringing. He counted along: four, five, six. He gave up, he knew it wouldn't stop. The cat leapt off the bed, arched its back and yawned.

He went to the phone that hung on the wall in the hallway, a black landline phone. He'd forgotten to pull out the plug. He answered. "Happy New Year," he said. "What time is it?"

He heard a faint chuckle. It was Corporal Lüdi. "Sorry to wake you. It's a quarter to nine."

"Well?" asked Hunkeler. He could hear loud bangs going off outside. It was the boys from the village, lighting fire-crackers on the street.

"What's all that racket in your peaceful Alsace?" asked Lüdi.

"A local New Year tradition. Come on, spill the beans. I want to get back to bed."

"I'm afraid that won't be possible. We're on call. And we need you."

"No," said Hunkeler. "Nobody needs me any more, apart from the cats and Hedwig. She needs me as a hot-water bottle. There's been a cold draught blowing in all night."

He could hear the chuckling again, miles away, as if from another continent. Hunkeler knew it didn't bode well. He felt the cold of the tiled floor against the soles of his feet, crawling up his legs and into his belly.

"Some get to lie in their warm beds and sleep off their

hangover, while others have to get on with the donkey work," said Lüdi.

"I'm exempt from work, special tasks only. Apparently my working methods are no longer tolerable. The chief public prosecutor personally said as much. You heard him yourself."

"True, you're probably no longer tolerable. But like I said, we need you."

There was another bang outside, right in front of his door. "Hang on," said Hunkeler. He tore open the front door and saw a group of boys run off.

"*Salauds*," he shouted, "bastards, little shits." Then he grinned. Job done, he knew what was good and proper. He, Inspector Hunkeler, in his nightshirt out in front of his house, scolding the cheeky brats. The snow-covered forecourt stretched out before him, with the boys' footprints all over it. In the cowshed across the road the lights were on, and he could hear the milking machine. The farmer was late up too this morning. He and his wife had probably been at Scholler's in Knoeringue until the early hours.

Hunkeler walked across to the walnut tree to relieve himself, then went back inside. He fetched a cigarette from the living room and lit it. He hadn't done this in years, first thing in the morning, on an empty stomach. Something was up, some kind of trouble, otherwise Lüdi wouldn't have woken him so early on New Year's Day.

"So, what's going on?" he asked when he had the receiver back in his hand.

"You know the allotments on Hegenheimerstrasse, right on the border. You pass them when you drive into Alsace."

"For God's sake, just get to the point."

9

"Each of those allotments has a small wooden cabin on it. You could sleep in those cabins, and at a pinch you could even live in them, but that's not allowed. In any case, they're all lovingly fitted out with little flags and all sorts of memorabilia. Luxury villas for the poor."

"What on earth are you waffling on about?" Hunkeler shouted. "If you're trying to build suspense, then say so. I'll go and have some breakfast first."

But Lüdi was undeterred. "Plot B35 has a particularly beautiful cabin. It looks like a pocket-sized Bernese chalet, really cosy. It's called Enzian. There's a flagpole out the front. It has a Bernese flag flying from it, the one with the bear. That's not permitted, as the allotments are on French territory."

Hunkeler waited. He knew he had no choice. Lüdi had to work himself up to things. It could be quite a protracted process at times.

"Are you still there?"

"Yes," said Hunkeler. "I've got all the time in the world."

"So, this cabin on plot B35 belongs to a man by the name of Anton Flückiger. He was formerly known as Anton Livius and was born in the former East Prussia, in Tilsit to be precise. We got that from the citizens' register. He came to Switzerland after the Second World War and was granted citizenship in Rüegsbach in the Emmental. He's over eighty, born in 1922. He lives at Dammerkirchstrasse in Basel, used to be a warehouse worker for a food retail chain, single, no descendants. He speaks in Bernese dialect. That's as much as we know for now."

"And why are you telling me this?"

"Paul Wirz is here, from the gendarmerie in Saint-Louis. He says he knows you."

"Of course we know each other, but what has Monsieur Wirz got to do with Anton Flückiger?"

He could hear Lüdi chuckling again, almost gloatingly. "A Monsieur François Bardet is on his way over. From Mulhouse. He asked for you straight away when he phoned."

The cold had now reached Hunkeler's innards. He was suddenly shivering. He desperately needed to get something warm, something hot, into his stomach. "Bardet," he said slowly. "He deals with murders."

"That's exactly what I'm driving at. This Anton Flückiger, alias Livius from Tilsit, was strung up last night."

"How do you mean, strung up?"

"He was shot first, in the forehead, at close range. Well, we're assuming this happened first. Then he was hung up with a meathook that someone had rammed under his chin and then attached to the beam above the door of Chalet Enzian. He was hanging there like a lump of meat."

Half an hour later, Hunkeler was sitting at the kitchen table. He was gazing out at the fog. At the snow-covered garden and the brown hens which he had let out. At the cherry tree and the willow. At the pear tree and the poplar, which were barely visible now. A female chaffinch fluttered onto the windowsill, pecked at a few grains that Hedwig had scattered there, briefly looked at the old man sitting at the table and flew off again.

He had made tea, and coffee for Hedwig. He'd lit a fire in the stove and listened to the crackling of the pine wood. Solemnly, he had eaten a yoghurt, and cheese and bread.

He'd done all this as slowly as possible, so that nothing would disturb the peaceful snowy morning. No fast movement, no clinking of cups.

First shot in the forehead, he thought, then hung up with a meathook. Or the other way around? First hung up, while alive? How could anyone do that? No, that was impossible. He would have fought back.

So, first the gunshot, which probably hadn't attracted any attention amid all the fireworks on New Year's Eve. Then the hanging up. But how do you hang up a dead man with a meathook? How many people would it take? Two or three?

Hunkeler topped up the food bowl for the cats. All they did was eat and sleep during these winter months. That was exactly what he'd been planning to do. And now it was probably off the table.

He lit a cigarette, took three drags then stubbed it out. He didn't want to start with that all over again, the damned smoking early in the morning. Darting around in a frenzy, puffing and panting in pursuit of unreliable leads. He wasn't going to let himself be drawn in again. No, not this time.

The door opened and Hedwig came in wearing her blue dressing gown. She padded to the table, sat down, poured herself some coffee, added a dash of milk and drank. She eyed him briefly, seemingly still half asleep. Then she refilled her mug. "What's up?" she asked.

"I have to go back into town. To the allotments at the border crossing to Hegenheim. An old man has been found hanging there."

She looked at him, mutely.

"Someone shot him and hung him up," he continued. "They found him this morning."

She cut herself a slice of bread, spread butter and honey on it, then chewed it very slowly. "We agreed that we wouldn't budge from the spot for the whole of the Christmas holidays. Just walks in the snowy forest, nothing else."

"Monsieur Bardet is coming over from Mulhouse," he said. "He wants to see me. I'm still in the service, I still draw a wage."

She dipped the knife into the jar, then carefully severed the thread of honey with a twist. He realized how much he liked her movements.

"In the past, when we'd arranged something, I used to be as excited as a child at Christmas," she told him. "For example ten days of hibernating in Hunkeler's house in Alsace. Cosy fires. Frost on the windows. Owls calling in the night. These days, I'm incapable of looking forward to anything. Because I know it won't come off."

"Stop it, will you?" he said with a harshness that surprised him.

"See?" she replied.

As he drove up the hill to the ridge road connecting Hésingue and Altkirch, he could feel the wheels spinning. There was ice under the snow. He grinned with satisfaction. A proper winter, this was.

At the top, by the St Imbert cross, he saw a body lying by the side of the road. He slammed on the brakes, he'd almost missed it. Carefully, he got out and approached it. It was a large, male badger that had been run over by someone. It was lying there as if asleep, the body perhaps still warm. Where its snout touched the snow, a patch of blood glowed red.

He left the animal where it was, got back in and drove on. A hunter would come by soon, they would know what to do with the carcass.

The visibility up on the ridge was so poor that he drove at walking pace. Nobody overtook him, nobody passed him, he seemed to be the only one out on the road. At Trois Maisons he looked across to the large, half-timbered house, wondering if the lights would be on. It was all dark.

He slowly rolled down the hill to Ranspach, in no hurry. He liked being enveloped in fog like this, it was like hiding out somewhere. He thought of the dead animal, Master Brock, whose luck had run out. The grey fur, the two stripes down the snout, the blood in the snow. Why had he left his sett? What was he looking for out in the cold? He'd lain on the embankment like an animal from a fairy tale.

Down on the plain the fog lifted. The snow on the fields was just inches deep here. There were no guards at the border crossing as he passed it. On the left was the gravel pit, now filled back in again, a white surface dotted with crows. To the right stood the storehouses of the building firms, dismantled cranes, trucks, yellow bulldozers. In front of him, the pale concrete gravel silo appeared, its conveyor belt cutting a diagonal line. It was a no man's land along the border, a historic absurdity in the twenty-first century. The gravel sat in French soil on the left, but was mined from Switzerland on the right. Also on his left were the allotments, cultivated by Swiss gardeners. A little further ahead, towards the city, was the Jewish cemetery.

He could see the cars from a distance. Several gendarmerie vehicles, a French ambulance, three Basel police cars, including one from the forensic department. There was also a French command vehicle, parked in a recess in the fence. Presumably that was still French soil.

Two gendarmes were guarding the allotment entrance. Probably local men. They were talking in Alsatian dialect to a group of angry allotment holders.

Hunkeler approached Haller, who was chewing on his pipe, looking uneasy. "Is Bardet here yet?"

"Yes," said Haller. "And Madame la Juge d'Instruction, Madeleine Godet. She arrived in the command vehicle. The contact man, Pierre Morath, and Paul Wirz from the Saint-Louis gendarmerie are also here. A whole lot of technicians too. And a journalist from *L'Alsace*. We're the only ones not allowed in. Happy New Year." He smiled bitterly, struck a match and lit his pipe. "Madörin is across the road in the Blume. He's livid, and also drunk. Lüdi is back at the station, searching through the various databases to see who this Anton Flückiger was. I reckon he's wasting his time. Every normal human being is still in bed on a morning like this."

"Where's Prosecutor Suter?"

"In Davos, at the Spengler Cup. He's an ice hockey fan. Didn't you know that?"

"Yes I did, but I'd forgotten," Hunkeler replied. "I've even forgotten that I'm a police officer."

Haller took the pipe out of his mouth and spat on the floor. "Listen, Hunki," he said. But Hunkeler had already turned away to cross the road.

On the right stood the Garten-Walther store, now closed. Planting anything was impossible, the ground was frozen solid. On the left stood a small brick building with a sign that read Stadtgärten-West. Perched between them was the Blume inn. It was a shack with an oil heater in the middle, a table reserved for the regulars on the left and a bar on the right. Card mats hung on the wall, and a large glass of Merlot cost 3.80. Evidently some sort of deal for the regulars, thought Hunkeler, judging by the cheapness of the wine.

The regulars' table was full. All older men, with a beer or coffee with schnapps in front of them. Another man, dressed in a purple jacket, was perched at the side table. He was wearing a Borsalino hat and talking on his phone in Italian.

Detective Sergeant Madörin was sitting in the corner at the back, a beer in his hand.

"What are you doing here?" Hunkeler asked.

"You can see what I'm doing. Getting drunk."

Hunkeler ordered coffee. "I've never seen you drink beer in the morning."

"What am I? The scum of the earth? Twenty-six years of service, and never missed a single day. Who do they think they are, those Alsatian halfwits? Is that Flückiger a Swiss man or not? Are these our people or not?" He looked up, a sad-eyed poodle that had been kicked in the behind. "I went to bed at four, with a fair amount of alcohol on board. At eight, Lüdi called and said someone was hanging from a rafter in the Stadtgärten-West allotments. I drove straight over, no breakfast. I was the first on the scene."

"Have you gone mad?" Hunkeler barked, causing everyone to turn and look. "Have you gone completely insane?"

"Why? He might have still been alive. The French ambulance didn't arrive until half eight. I heard it from miles away and disappeared."

"If that gets out, we'll be in all sorts of trouble," said Hunkeler. "They don't like people poking their noses into their business. The allotments are French territory. The gendarmerie or the Police Nationale are responsible. But certainly not you."

"Exactly. That's why I'm getting drunk. What do I care who strung the guy up? I'm going to drive over to Kleinbasel now and join the winos in the Schwarzer Bären." He ordered another beer.

"You'd better be careful," said Hunkeler. "You're on duty."

"Is that so?"

Hunkeler indicated a bald-headed man at the regulars' table. "Who's that over there? Do you know him?"

"Who?"

"The fat one with the bald head. He nodded at me."

"What's it to me?"

Hunkeler stirred two sugars into his coffee. He did it nice and slowly, he needed time to think.

"I spent Christmas in the Emmental," Madörin told him. "Together with my wife. We stayed with our daughter. She rents a house there all year round. She wants her kids to experience rural life so they don't become completely urbanized. And now this."

"And now what?"

"Somebody rammed a meathook into his chin. They nearly tore his head off doing it. And there's not much left of the forehead. The shot must have been fired at close range." He lifted his gaze, he looked harrowed, full of

17

despair. "What kind of job is this? Can you tell me? There I am, spending peaceful days in the Emmental. Just snow and wind and pine forests. And then this."

Hunkeler had gathered his thoughts. "Look, my friend," he said. "We're both members of the Basel police department. We stick together, even if we shout at each other sometimes. Desertion is not an option. Understood?"

Madörin nodded. "Thanks."

"And now one step at a time. Was the man still hanging there when you arrived?"

"First I need another beer."

"No. Coffee." Hunkeler waved at the waitress and ordered coffee.

Madörin shook his head a couple of times, then he was ready. "There were two pensioners at the scene. Martin Füglistaller and Jürg Stebler. They had spent the night in the neighbouring cabin. They took him down. Then they phoned, Lüdi answered. He called me and the French ambulance and then looked in the citizens' directory. It seems the man was originally from East Prussia."

"Slow down, one thing at a time. I didn't get to bed until three myself."

Madörin lifted the coffee cup with shaking hands and drank. "OK. I parked the car and went in. The gate had been left open. I didn't see anyone. There were only a few tracks in the snow. Two looked to be from a man and a woman or child. They'd walked beside each other to the exit. Apart from that, the snow was untouched."

"Did you see where those two tracks came from?"

"Yes. They came from plot B26. Plot B26 is to the left, plot B35 to the right and further back. There were lots of tracks round there, across to plots B37 and B39. There were also tracks that led towards Alsace. I didn't pay much attention to them. Füglistaller and Stebler were about to take down the Bernese flag on B35 when I turned up. The deceased was lying crosswise on the stone slabs in front of the door. He was on his back, dressed in a blue tracksuit. The blood was no longer flowing, but the stone slabs were covered in it. There was no snow there – the patio has a roof over it. The hook was lying next to his head. The door was open. Those two idiots had been stomping around in the cabin and all over the patio. The only thing I was able to determine was that someone had pissed into the snow next to the wrapped-up rose bush. And that this someone was a barefooted man."

"And inside the cabin?"

"That's where there was the most blood. I saw the bullet hole, in the wall facing north. It's a thin wooden wall, the shot had penetrated it cleanly."

"Had anybody spent the night in the cabin?"

"Yes, definitely. On a fold-up bed. It was toppled over. The quilt was lying on the floor. It was odd that the quilt had a red and white chequered cover. My grandmother used to have those covers."

"Strange," said Hunkeler. "An old man with a colourful past, who has built himself a cosy little slice of Emmental, is slaughtered like a rabbit."

"That's not all," Madörin continued, and it was clear he'd talked himself back into his job, like a fierce, tough little terrier. "Everything there indicated that it had been a long night. The folding bed was tipped on its side, one of the chairs was lying on the floor. There were two empty beer bottles and three glasses on the table, beside them a bottle of Chianti, nearly empty. There was also a box of painkillers and a water glass with remnants of a white powder in it. I didn't have much time, of course, but I definitely saw that."

"That's good." Hunkeler nodded approvingly.

"Stop it, will you. Don't take the piss."

"What do you mean?"

But Madörin pushed it aside. He was on a roll now. "There were some postcards stuck to the wall on the right, all of them from Thailand. And several photos of Thai beauties, all naked."

"Well, well," commented Hunkeler. "Bit of a playboy then."

"Next to them was a medicine cabinet, white with a red cross on it. The floor below was scattered with medicines, the cabinet was empty. I had a quick look at what was lying there. Blood pressure tablets, vitamin tablets, magnesium. Two packets of condoms."

"He kept himself in shape, successfully it seems," said Hunkeler.

"Yes, but something was missing."

"What?"

"Well, what do you think?"

"Oh, the Viagra."

"There you go." Madörin now had the upper hand and he was enjoying it. "I searched through his trouser pockets. Nothing. Eventually I found them in his left jacket pocket. Here they are." He placed the box on the table.

"Are you crazy?" shouted Hunkeler. "That's misappropriation of evidence."

"I don't care. I wore gloves."

"That could cost you your job."

"Nonsense. It's their own fault for arriving late."

Hunkeler slammed his coffee cup on the table so hard it nearly shattered. "What the hell were you thinking?" he roared. "How can we explain this?" He lit a cigarette and pulled the smoke deep into his lungs. Then, very quietly: "A Basel detective trampling around on a French crime scene. It's the perfect scandal."

"Not true. I didn't trample, I crept."

"Is that so? And the two old guys, Füglistaller and Stebler? They probably saw you."

"That's possible. But they'll keep quiet. They had guilty consciences."

"Why?"

"I don't know. But they were hiding something from me, that much was clear."

"What? What were they hiding?"

Madörin shrugged. "No idea. They were up to something, I'm sure of that. Füglistaller still had the flag in his hand when I got out of there."

"Didn't they run off with you?"

"No. Stebler said they wanted to hold vigil for a while longer. Will you pay for my coffee?"

Hunkeler thought of the badger lying in the snow. Of the blood that had caused the snow to melt around the snout. Had the animal crawled onto the embankment by itself, using its last bit of strength to save itself? Or had the driver dragged it off the road? Had he been able to drive away, just like that, after the heavy impact?

And what time had it stopped snowing this morning? When he was chugging home with Hedwig, after three, the air had still been full of snowflakes.

Madörin, who had arrived at the crime scene shortly after eight, had seen two tracks, from a woman and a man. They'd led from plot B26 to the exit. So those two people had probably left the allotments after three. Or perhaps it had stopped snowing earlier down here than it had up on the Hohe Strasse.

He stood up, went over to the regulars' table and sat down on a free chair. "May I?"

"But of course, Herr Hunkeler," replied the bald-headed man. "We know each other already."

"Do we?"

"Yes, I'm a neighbour. I live on Mittlere Strasse too. I often see you when you go jogging in Kannenfeld Park. My name is Cattaneo, Ettore Cattaneo."

"Oh yes, I remember now. You have a wife, don't you? A petite, jolly woman."

"No, she died." A haze passed across the man's eyes, like a veil of mist, a watery film. He was in his late seventies, stocky, with a red, swollen face. Three-day beard, white stubble. He was wearing a warm casual shirt, black and white checked, and a padded jacket. His heavy shoes had left wet marks on the parquet floor, prints of rubber soles with a mountaineering profile.

"Oh, I see, I'm sorry," Hunkeler replied.

"That was four years ago. Life goes on, I'm in love with someone new."

"Congratulations."

"Thank you. We get along well. May I introduce you to these gentlemen?"

"Please. If you don't mind, I'll jot down the names." He pulled out his notebook, the one with the blue graph paper. He looked at the men. Old fellows with lined faces and heavy hands. Two of them, widowers, wore double wedding rings. All of them looked unshaven and bleary-eyed. "Why are you sitting here instead of lying in your beds?" he asked.

"Beat heard about it on Radio Basilisk," Cattaneo explained. "He rang some of us. We want to know what's going on in the allotments."

"And the others?"

"A few had spent the night there. As an exception, because it was New Year's Eve. What's the situation, if I may ask? Are you leading the investigation? Or is it Paul Wirz from Saint-Louis, or that pompous snob from Mulhouse? What's his name again?"

"Bardet," said the man next to him. "I've never met anyone so arrogant. We're to remain available, he said. For how long? And who's in charge here anyway?"

"This Anton Flückiger, what sort of person was he?" Hunkeler asked.

"He was one of us," replied Cattaneo. "Is it true that they tore his head off?"

"One step at a time," said Hunkeler. "Nice and slowly, please." He took out his pen and noted down what he heard.

Werner Siegrist, stationery shop owner on Blumenrain, chair of the Stadtgärten-West allotment association. The one who asked who was in charge here. Thick white hair. Coffee with cream.

Matthyas Schläpfer, graphic designer, Bachlettenstrasse, vice chair, double wedding ring. Coffee with schnapps.

Rudolf Pfeifer, carpenter, Lothringerstrasse. Double wedding ring. Black tea.

Beat Pfister, antiquarian and bric-a-brac trader, Hegenheimerstrasse. Wedding ring. Coffee with schnapps.

All retired, Hunkeler noted, everyday folk, respectable members of the public. "Hang on," he said, "I forgot something. What was your line of work?"

Ettore Cattaneo, he wrote, laboratory assistant, Mittlere Strasse. New partner, therefore without ring. Coffee with schnapps.

"So, what now?" Siegrist asked. "Is there even any point writing this stuff down, seeing as it isn't you conducting the investigation?"

"As the allotments are on French territory, the Saint-Louis gendarmerie is in charge," Hunkeler explained. "In murder cases, it's the Police Nationale Judiciaire in Mulhouse. As the victim was a Swiss citizen, Mulhouse will work with the Basel criminal investigation department. For these situations, there is a contact man. His name is Pierre Morath, he lives in Village Neuf and has an office at the Spiegelhof station. The Police Nationale will issue a mutual assistance request and the public prosecutor will respond to it. It will all sort itself out. By the way, it was two Swiss allotment holders who found the deceased. Füglistaller and Stebler. Has anyone seen them this morning?"

They thought about this for a long time. They scratched their heads, they rubbed their chins. Sips of beer and coffee were taken.

"Has anyone seen them?" Schläpfer asked. "Not me, I haven't seen them."

They all shook their heads, nobody had seen them.

Hunkeler waited, let them stew a while. "I was under the impression that several people had spent the night on their allotments and celebrated together," he then said.

"Did any of you spend the night in the allotments?" Siegrist asked.

No, nobody had spent the night in the allotments.

"I heard that Füglistaller and Stebler's cabins are right next to B35," Hunkeler persisted. "Is that correct?"

"Yes, Füglistaller has B37 and Stebler has B39," Siegrist replied. "All you need to do is look at the plot map, it's all on there."

"Exactly. I understand that you want to protect your friends. But this isn't the way to do it."

"OK," said Siegrist, "you'll find out anyway. Füglistaller kept rabbits on his plot, although that's frowned upon. Keeping small animals is permitted, provided the keeper is a member of a pet owners' association. And he is. Anyway, he's not the only one. Beat Pfister here keeps ducks."

"That's right," Pfister chimed in. "And my ducks have a good life."

"Füglistaller loved his rabbits, so he never ate them himself. He usually killed two at a time. He hung them up on meathooks and skinned them. Then he gave them away for free. This all worked perfectly fine, until early December. Or when was it?"

"No," said Pfister, "it was more like mid-December. It was already cold. We'd had the first snowfall. Anyway, that Sunday, he found all fourteen of the rabbits dead in front of his cabin. All laid out together. They were handsome Swiss Spotteds, with good soft fur. All killed with a blow to the neck. The animals could easily still have been eaten, but Füglistaller wouldn't give them to anyone. He buried them all in the garden, even though that's not allowed."

"It was OK," Siegrist corrected. "The hole was deep enough."

"Who do you think killed the animals?" Hunkeler asked.

"No idea," said Siegrist.

Hunkeler waited a while. Then he closed his notebook and slid it into his pocket. It was obvious he wasn't going to get much else out of them. "Just one more thing," he said. "Is there something like an allotment rule book?"

Siegrist nodded without looking up. "The landlady has a copy."

"Well then," Hunkeler said cheerfully. "We're bound to see each other again soon." He went over to the bar to pay.

"It's OK," said the landlady. "The bill's already been settled. Here's the community allotment rule book." She pointed at the pamphlet she'd placed on the bar.

The cluster of people outside was bigger now; word about the murder had got around. People fell silent when they saw him coming. They looked at him with angry eyes.

"Finally," one of them said. "Finally one of the Basel cops has turned up. Where have you been? Sleeping on the job?

D'you think we want to leave it to those French clowns to solve this murder? He was one of us."

Hunkeler stopped and took a close look at the man. He was around seventy, stockily built, in a green hunting jacket.

"I'm the elected grounds warden here. Walter Widmer is my name. The allotment holders are strictly required to follow my orders. And by the way, it's forbidden to carry a firearm in the allotments."

"Of course," said Hunkeler. "Everything is forbidden in the allotments, isn't it?"

"Are you taking the piss?"

"Of course not. Why would I be?" He pushed the man aside and joined Haller. "Has fat Hauser been here?"

"No, not yet."

"If you need backup, call in. There must be a few out on patrol."

"I've already called several times. Everyone was on duty into the early hours." Haller elaborately tapped out his pipe. "Can you imagine how many people it would take to seal off the whole allotment area? Twenty or thirty probably."

"But don't let fat Hauser in. Not this time."

"If he wants to get in, he can climb over the fence somewhere."

The morning mist had cleared and it was noticeably warmer, but a bank of heavy clouds hovered over the western horizon. The concrete tower of the gravel quarry loomed on the left, with the dark band of the Vosges mountains visible further north. The gravestones of the Jewish cemetery could be seen through the fence on the right and behind them the chimney of the waste incineration plant. In the distance, the outstretched mountains of the Black Forest were bathed in sunshine. An odd contrast. Must be the föhn wind coming over the Alps, or perhaps a warm westerly from the sea?

Hunkeler walked along Roggenburgstrasse. To the left and right stood blocks of apartments, five storeys high, with large windows and playgrounds outside. Swings, slide, the usual stuff. He had lived in that kind of apartment for a time, over on Markircherstrasse, with his wife and his daughter Isabelle. It was years since he'd last seen her.

The sky had blackened, dark clouds were now hovering over the city and it started to snow again. Not softly and quietly, no dancing flakes. This was something between hail and sleet, he supposed. It pattered down, and he pulled up his hood.

Further along, by the bend, stood the play barn of the adventure playground. He'd been there a couple of times, with his daughter. It was many years ago, or had he dreamed it? Now, on this New Year's Day morning, the barn appeared to be empty. Next to it was the practice room of Cannibal Frost, a heavy metal band everyone at the CID department was well-acquainted with. Breach of the peace, time and again. The tenants in the surrounding apartments had forced through a 10 p.m. curfew on band practice. But the youngsters were only just getting started then. Endless accusations of criminal damage. If something in the area had been broken or stolen, it was blamed on the Cannibals.

Hunkeler knew the band a little. He quite liked the lads. But their music was too loud for him. The room seemed to be unoccupied now, he couldn't see any lights. Perhaps it was just because of the sleet. It was hammering down so hard you couldn't see more than twenty yards.

As he crossed Hegenheimerstrasse towards the Luzernerring Restaurant, a small car came racing towards him. He saved himself with a leap onto the sidewalk. It was fat Hauser, the fastest camera in Basel. He was out and about for Zurich's tabloid press.

Hunkeler stopped and watched the car disappear. Had he really been the kind of father who took his young daughter to the adventure playground, he wondered. No, he hadn't, he'd just dreamed it. He grinned bitterly. He couldn't change his past, only the way he remembered it.

He looked back at the barn, almost wistfully. Some of the tree houses the kids had built were still clinging on among the branches.

Hunkeler went into the bar and sat down at a table on the right. The place had a bright and cheery air to it, a sort of Sundayish vibe. Today was in fact Sunday, he realized. A Sunday New Year's Day. The tables were wiped clean and a fire crackled in the tiled stove. A few streamers hanging from the lamps were all that was left of last night's celebrations.

Mara came to the table and asked what he would like. Originally from the former Yugoslavia, she'd waited tables here for more than thirty years. He'd often wanted to ask her whether she came from Serbia, Croatia or Kosovo. He never had though, it would have made him feel stupid.

He ordered water. He felt thirsty, probably an after-effect of the Crémant d'Alsace. "It's nice you're open so early on New Year's Day," he said.

"We've been open since nine," she replied. "The landlord has only been here for six months, he's still making an effort." She remained standing by his table, adjusting her hair. "Why are you here?" she asked. "Are you involved with the murder in the allotments?"

"Yes, but not directly. It's on French territory."

"Is it true he was beheaded?"

"Who says that?"

"I listened to Radio Basilisk. I knew Toni Flückiger well."

"Did you?"

"He lived just round the corner, on Dammerkirchstrasse. He was a regular here. He always sat back there in the alcove."

"What did he drink?"

"Armagnac. Always just the one. Served in a brandy glass. Nobody else here drinks Armagnac. We kept a bottle just for him." She readjusted her hairdo, coyly. Her hair had turned grey, he noticed, but her charm remained.

"You liked him, did you?" he commented.

She nodded. "He was a ladies' man. Women liked him. Sometimes he would sit there for over an hour, without talking to anyone. I would have liked to help him, but he didn't want to be helped. Sometimes he sat and wrote."

"Wrote what?"

"Postcards. Picture postcards of Basel Minster and the Rhine."

"Did you see who they were addressed to?"

"No, I didn't want to be rude. I left him in peace."

"What did he talk like?"

"He spoke in a very broad Bernese dialect, rural I guess. But he looked out of place somehow. Out of place in his skin, out of place here in Basel. I could tell straight away, I'm a foreigner too."

"And why are you telling me this?"

"Because I need to talk to someone about it. He never hurt a fly." She looked at him again, almost pleadingly. Then she went back to the bar. He watched her as she walked away. Strange, he thought, she hasn't aged. How has she managed that? Armagnac? Why Armagnac? How had Anton Flückiger come to drink such a posh French tipple?

At the regulars' table across the room, a youngish man sat with his head bent forward, a beer in front of him. He seemed to be sleeping. He had his hat beside him on the table.

Hunkeler took out the allotment rule book and started to read. *The area occupied by the Stadtgärten-West allotments is leased by the Basel City buildings department,* it said. *The National Allotments Commission is responsible for the orderly running of the grounds. It is the commission's role to conclude a contract of lease with the allotment holders. The executive body is the Department for Community Allotments.*

Reasons for instant termination of the lease contract include acts of violence, weed infestation and general disorderliness.

The following cabin types are desirable: chalet, chalet with integrated porch, cabin with sloped roof, cabin with gable roof. Length 11 feet, width 8 feet, height 9 feet from highest point of the terrain.

One lean-to pergola with or without roof is permitted per allotment. Pergolas without a roof may also be free-standing. The supports must not consist of more than one supporting beam.

A screen made of natural bamboo canes may be attached to one side. Old, unattractive bamboo screens must be promptly removed. The roof structure must be designed horizontally. Gabled shapes are not permitted.

Per allotment, one water lily pond may be installed, with a maximum surface area of 65 square feet and a maximum depth of 30 inches. Children's paddling pools with a depth of more than 2 feet are not permitted.

Cultivation must be in accordance with organic horticultural methods.

Neighbouring gardens must not be affected by windborne seed dissemination. In the event of pervasive weed encroachment, the supervising bodies may intervene.

The installation of a garden barbecue is permitted. The overall height above ground (incl. flue) must not exceed 7 feet.

The following are prohibited:

– Keeping small animals, with the exception of rabbits and chickens, provided the keeper is a member of a relevant breeders' association.

– Continuous dog barking.

– The feeding of cats.

– Overnight stays in the cabins.

– The selling of garden produce.

– Firearms.

The area ranger has authorization to cull wild animals.

Instructions issued by the grounds warden must strictly be complied with.

Odd, thought Hunkeler, people go and build their bit of paradise, and the first thing they do is draw up a list of everything that's banned. But then wasn't it the same in the biblical Paradise? Hadn't there been a strict rule regarding the apple tree? It was a good thing Eve didn't stick to it. Otherwise humankind would still be dancing in circles singing "Ring-a-ring-o' roses".

He was fed up. He didn't give a damn about those blasted community allotments. But why had Anton Flückiger been hung up with a meathook? You could understand a bit of night-time sawing at the neighbour's pergola in protest against unwanted shade. Or a blow with an axe to sabotage a sprawling lily pond. Perhaps even a few lead pellets in the behind as payback for a heavy windborne weed infestation. But who would first shoot a man in the head point-blank and then hang him from a roof beam? Would an angry allotment holder defending their territory go that far?

Hunkeler didn't think so. Shooting someone, that was conceivable, yes. Pulling the trigger on someone, straight in the nut, once and for all, so there'd be peace at last. But the meathook?

No, the meathook was about something more. It was a sign of something. Something very particular. It indicated intent, a story.

He lit a cigarette and greedily pulled the smoke into his lungs. He was aware of the greed, but it didn't bother him. Not right now. He was still addicted, even though he often didn't smoke for days in a row. The craving remained. It would be with him as long as he lived. The craving for nicotine. The craving for stories.

Hunkeler looked at the man sleeping at the table across the room. He hadn't touched his beer yet, he'd probably bought it just in case.

"Does anyone know when it stopped snowing this morning?" Hunkeler asked the empty room.

"No," replied Mara, who was lining up glasses behind the bar. "I went home just before three. It was still snowing heavily then."

The young man across the room lifted his head. He reached for his glass, raised it with both hands and slowly brought it to his lips. He remained that way for a while, letting the beer wet his tongue. Then he began to sip, carefully, as if something might break. He drank his beer like a baby drinking its milk.

"Over in Kleinbasel it was snowing at midnight," the man across the room said. "That's when I went across to the Alte Schluuch. I know it was midnight because all the bells in the city were ringing. At half two I moved on to the Klingenthal. It was still snowing then. Around six I went to the Schiefen Eck. It wasn't snowing any more by then. But the roads were covered in snow, you could see every track."

The sleet had stopped when Hunkeler stepped out onto the road, but the wind was fierce. It tugged at the tree branches, which dropped their load of snow then bounced upwards.

He thought about going straight to his car and driving back to Alsace. Hedwig was probably sitting at the kitchen table right now, wondering what to do with herself on this New Year's Day.

The Hegenheim church clock over in Alsace struck twelve as Hunkeler arrived back at the allotments. First four bright peals, then another twelve, deep and slow, carried across by the westerly. It had started to rain.

Reinforcement had arrived for Haller. Sergeant Kaelin from the Basel cantonal police with his patrol colleagues.

"Good that you're back," said Kaelin. "It's all gone haywire here."

"What? What's gone haywire?"

"Nobody knows what to do. Our technical support unit drove off half an hour ago. And how are we supposed to guard the entire allotment area with three officers?"

"How much sleep have you had?"

"Just under two hours. But that doesn't matter. We're ready and operational, if they'll let us."

"I think it's best if you go and get some sleep," Hunkeler decided. "We have to wait for the mutual assistance request. I imagine it'll come through sometime today. Then we'll have to get cracking."

"OK," said Kaelin. "We'll head off." He got back into the car with his colleagues and drove off towards the city.

Hunkeler joined Haller, who was standing next to two Alsatian gendarmes, chatting. "Go home," Hunkeler told him. "We're not wanted here right now."

"I agree," replied Haller. "But it's strange. It seems there was a full-blown New Year's Eve party in the allotments last night, with loads of fireworks. Quite a few spent the night in their cabins. But nobody's in there any more, and nobody knows anything. We're not allowed in, and the French aren't allowed into Basel. How's that going to work?" He sucked on his pipe, but it had gone out. "By the way, Suter's coming back. The briefing is at four."

Hunkeler looked across to the French command vehicle. The lights were on inside. He would have liked to go over there and talk to Bardet, but he didn't have clearance for that. A westerly gust almost swept his hood off his head, he could feel the heavy rain thrumming on his back. The glare of the floodlights could be seen hovering above the allotments. This weather must be making it immensely difficult to assess the crime scene and secure any evidence.

Hunkeler drove to Mittlere Strasse and parked. He emptied his letter box and climbed the stairs to his apartment on the second floor. He chucked the junk mail in the wastepaper basket, sat down at the kitchen table and called Hedwig. The line was engaged.

What should he do? Look for Füglistaller and Stebler? He searched in the phone book and found their names. But he didn't have authorization. He briefly switched on the television and listened to a few bars of a waltz performed by the Vienna Philharmonic. No, that wasn't right just now. He needed to clear his head, get some distance from what had happened. Dancing into the night with Hedwig, driving home through the snowy night. Then the sudden waking, being told about the murder, immersing him in a world he hadn't sought or wanted. But that was his job, he was also a victim of the perpetrators.

He went back out and walked towards the city. There was barely anyone about. The snow, now wet and heavy, slid off the parked cars, the gutters were full of water. He crossed Petersplatz and turned off into the Heuberg quarter with its medieval houses. The old buildings looked as if they had grown organically, each different to the next yet forming a comforting whole. In some parts, Basel was a beautiful city.

He descended the steps to Barfüsserplatz. A tram stopped and opened its doors. Three people got out, nobody got in. The doors closed and the tram pulled away, its green emanating a surreal glow in the rain. Taxis stood here and there, waiting for customers. The drivers seemed to be sleeping.

He passed the Rio Bar and poked his head through the door. He saw two men he knew from the old days. Each sat alone, each with a beer in front of him. He wondered if he should go in and join them. He decided to leave it.

The Steinenvorstadt quarter was empty too. Beer cans and broken bottles littered the ground, some of the tables and chairs must have been toppled by the wind. Or perhaps a few youngsters had had a bit of fun going on the rampage.

He didn't care. He steered towards the high-rise and took the elevator up to Harry's sauna. He sat in the steam and perspired briefly and heavily, three times in quick succession, dousing himself with cold water in between. Then he went up to the roof terrace. He laid down on his back and felt the rain falling on his belly.

When he woke up, he felt better. He was cold, almost shivering, the way he used to feel as a youngster when he'd stayed in the cool water for a long time. It was still raining, the snow on the terrace had melted. He stepped up to the railing and looked down at the crossing and the cars rolling over the viaduct with their headlights on.

He sat at the bar for a good half hour, drank a pot of tea, no sugar, and ate a croque-monsieur – crisp slices of toast with ham and molten cheese between them. He chatted to Harry about the weather that had changed so quickly this morning, and about the Spengler Cup in Davos, which had been won by the Russian team. By the time he left the sauna, he'd almost forgotten about the allotments.

At the reception desk of Waaghof police station, Frau Held welcomed him with a radiant smile. She was old-fashioned, which Hunkeler liked. Her white blouse was adorned with a red coral necklace.

"How do you manage it?" asked Hunkeler. "Even on a sopping wet New Year's Day you sparkle like a Christmas tree."

She wagged a warning finger at him. "You old devil, you smooth-talking charmer."

It was the same as always when he returned to his workplace after a few days in Alsace. He stood in the elevator like a stranger, watching trance-like as the floor numbers flashed up one by one. He walked along the corridor feeling oddly detached from himself.

The team was already assembled when he entered the room. Dr de Ville, Alsatian and head of the forensic department, had a strange pallor about him. Perhaps he was feeling sick. Or he'd pulled an all-nighter.

Madörin wasn't there.

The French contingent was led by Commissaire Bardet from Mulhouse, who sat at a table with his hat in front of him. Also from Mulhouse was Madame Madeleine Godet, Juge d'Instruction from the Police Nationale Judiciaire, a small, youngish woman with horn-rimmed glasses, and contact man Pierre Morath, a young man from Village Neuf, with a stern gaze behind his metal-rimmed spectacles.

Prosecutor Suter was wearing a bright yellow ski jumper over a shirt of purest white. The tan on his face spoke of exhilarating ski runs down snowy slopes. It was immediately evident that his exemplary sense of duty had torn him out of his well-earned winter holidays. "Good," he said with a painfully resolute expression. "We can finally make a start."

His speech was another one of his rhetorical masterpieces. He started off by talking about the humble, honest man's yearning for a piece of home, a patch of his own, no matter how small. Switzerland was, after all, a nation of farmers. A confederation founded by herders and dairymen. This heritage, he said, remained deeply rooted within each and every one. He had himself experienced this profoundly while in Davos, surrounded by the snow-covered peaks. Although Davos had long grown into a town, favoured by the great and the good of the world, its character was still defined by the Grisons dialect and by the rustic mountain people. This had been most particularly apparent up in the ski huts as they shared a bottle of Veltliner before the last descent to the valley in the evening's waning light.

That was what made Switzerland so great. This diversity within unity. On the one hand you had the mountain farmers who spent their summers looking after cattle and producing cheese. On the other you had the upstanding Anton Flückigers who'd worked in a warehouse all their lives. Alpine hut there, allotment cabin here. The difference wasn't as big as it seemed. After all, hadn't the warehouse worker Flückiger named his little cabin Enzian, in honour of the blue flower so characteristic of the Alps? City here, countryside there, united in the blue symbol of reconciliatory confederate loyalty.

What a pity there were no TV cameras present, thought Hunkeler. This would have made an outstanding New Year's Day address.

"But let's not forget that we live in Europe," Suter went on. "Let us try to stretch this blue band a little further, beyond the narrow confines of our national border. Basel, perhaps more than any other Swiss city, is historically predestined to make that step across the border. Let us remember that our neighbouring city Mülhausen was once an allied town of the Swiss Confederation. The confederate heraldry can still be seen on Mülhausen's town hall today. I am therefore particularly delighted to be welcoming three representatives from Alsace to our meeting.

"What has happened? A law-abiding Swiss citizen, an upstanding pensioner, has been murdered in one of Basel's community allotments. Terrible. What can I say? This deed must not remain unpunished. If the common citizen is no longer safe in their own four walls, the very foundations of our community threaten to collapse. I am determined to solve this murder at all costs. I am declaring it a matter of highest importance.

"We know that the crime occurred on French soil. Therefore, the Police Nationale is responsible. I would like to stress that we have complete faith in the French investigative bodies. And, as loyal neighbours, we hereby extend an emphatic offer of help."

Prosecutor Suter sat down, seemingly exhausted. He pushed a finger between his shirt collar and neck to get some air.

Bardet had lit a cigarette during the speech, even though smoking wasn't permitted. "Aren't there any ashtrays here?" he asked. Lüdi ran out to get one.

"*Merci*, Monsieur le Procureur," said Bardet. "*Merci* for this *discours patriotique*. It is the first of January today, a day on which it is of course customary to address the nation. By the way, how did you find out that Monsieur Flückiger's cabin is called Enzian?"

Suter rubbed his chin. Then he seemed to remember.

"Corporal Lüdi told me. I had a long telephone conversation with him. Why?"

"No reason. What I want to tell you is that Mulhouse is still called Mulhouse and hasn't been referred to as Mülhausen for a long time. And something else: you can shove your blue Enzian you know where."

Suter kept his poise. The tan on his face rapidly faded to a pallor that looked oddly out of place against the yellow jumper. Then he smiled sweetly. "Did I hear you correctly, Monsieur?" he asked. "Did you perhaps strike the wrong tone just now?"

"That's possible. But you adopted a very peculiar tone yourself a moment ago."

"*Mais restez tranquilles, Messieurs,*" intervened Madame Godet. "Let's try and remain calm. We have to work together, whether we like it or not. I suggest we get down to business."

"Agreed, we're ready," Suter replied.

"Good. I would like to thank Prosecutor Suter for meeting our request for mutual assistance so promptly. I'm glad we were able to sort everything out over the phone. The documents and signatures will be provided shortly. We find ourselves in a difficult position with this case. We will of course be carrying out all technical aspects of the investigation, including the autopsy. But we can't get to the people, the possible perpetrators, as all the allotments are leased by Basel citizens."

"It's also possible that the perpetrators are from Alsace," Suter interjected.

"Correct, that could be the case. We will of course be looking into that possibility too. As you see, there are three of us here. Pierre Morath, whom you already know, is our contact man. Monsieur Bardet you're also familiar with. And I probably don't need to introduce my humble self either." She attempted a charming smile, which came off quite well. "Prosecutor Suter has authorized us to play an active part in any important interrogations and investigations. We won't be doing these on our own, but together with Basel investigators. Isn't that right, Mr Prosecutor?"

"That's right, all in accordance with the Switzerland–France treaty," Suter replied.

"Good. First of all, we'd be interested in finding out who was at the crime scene. There were two older men present when the ambulance arrived. After a brief discussion, they left without giving their names."

"I'd be interested in finding out why the ambulance took so long to arrive," Hunkeler commented.

"It's true, the ambulance did arrive late," Bardet agreed. "It was due to a serious accident in Rosenau, caused by black ice."

"The two men are Martin Füglistaller, residing at Wanderstrasse, and Jürg Stebler, residing at Allschwilerstrasse," said Hunkeler. "Regulars at the Blume gave me their names."

"Is that so?" commented Bardet and smiled in an overly affable manner. "You've been making enquiries, then?"

"Of course."

"It seems that a third person was also prowling around the crime scene," Bardet continued. "We found their tracks. They even entered the cabin and tampered with the victim's clothes. Do you know the name of this person too?"

"No, we don't know that yet."

Bardet smiled again and gave a friendly nod. "And how is it that so many people spent the night in the allotments, even though that isn't permitted?" he asked.

"That will form part of our inquiry," replied Hunkeler. "It may be that the heavy snowfall prevented people from going home. When did it stop snowing, anyway?"

"At 3.42 a.m.," said Lüdi. "I called the meteorological station."

"Yes, of course," Bardet said sweetly. "The heavy snowfall. First it covers all the tracks. Then a couple of idiots trample all over the crime scene. And finally, a strong westerly and heavy rain sweep away any remaining traces." He slammed his fist on the table so hard it made the ashtray jump. "How on earth are we supposed to carry out an investigation like this?"

"Are you trying to suggest that we're responsible for the weather?" Suter asked.

Bardet shook his head, several times in succession, then composed himself. He lit another cigarette and tried to smile. "Apologies. I'm not used to dealing with border-related obstructions like these. And I haven't had enough sleep."

"Right," said Madame Godet. "Let's get started. All strings of the investigation will come together in our command vehicle. At least for the time being, until we've found better premises. That is imperative."

"Of course," Suter agreed.

"Good. The technical investigations will take time. We'll inform you immediately when we have any results. Who is our contact for this?"

"Corporal Lüdi will be available in his office."

"Not always, but most of the time," said Lüdi. "You can also reach me on my mobile phone."

"I will want to be in touch with Inspector Hunkeler," Bardet said. "We've worked together successfully in the past."

"The first thing we should do is take a closer look at the two men," said Madame Godet. "What were their names again?"

"Füglistaller and Stebler," replied Hunkeler. With that, the meeting was closed. As they left the room, Hunkeler took Bardet by the arm. "Are you staying locally?"

"I don't know," Bardet replied. "I'll certainly need a room for the next few nights."

"Hotel au Violon, at the former Lohnhof prison," Hunkeler suggested. "Centrally located and very pleasant. Go have a look. I'll pick you up from there in an hour."

"OK," said Bardet.

They had the greatest trouble calming Prosecutor Suter down after the French delegation had left the building. "The impertinence!" he yelled. He wasn't going to tolerate being treated like that by those damn Alsatians, those imbeciles. He didn't have to put up with that kind of attitude. He was going to drive straight back to Davos. See how they managed then, those arrogant upstarts. He wasn't going to have anything more to do with them. There was no question, he felt offended, upstanding Basel citizen that he was. He prided himself on his rhetorical skills, which had served him so well in his career.

It was only when Lüdi put to him what kind of headlines his absence might provoke in Zurich's tabloid press – "Basel prosecutor enjoys the good life" – that he decided to stay in Basel.

Hunkeler retreated to his office. He sat down on the stained oak chair he'd brought in from home and gazed at the scraps of paper piled up on his desk. They were his principal tool. Amid them stood the computer he hardly ever used. The others did; Lüdi, for example, was a real IT hotshot. No doubt he'd already fired up the machinery and was printing out countless reports and lists. Nothing would come of it in the end, apart from full wastepaper baskets and a bit of hot air.

He reached for the telephone and called Madörin. He got the answer machine. "Cut the boozing, we need you tomorrow, Monday," he said onto the recording.

Carefully, he placed his feet against the edge of the desk, first the left one, then the right. He tipped the chair backwards until he was perfectly balanced. He laid his hands on his knees and curled himself over so his head touched his hands. He remained that way for several minutes, taking slow breaths, as if he loved his head. But it wasn't his head he loved, just this position. He knew it wouldn't help him land on any new ideas. What ideas, anyway? He knew nothing.

He went over to see Lüdi. "What do you know about Anton Flückiger?" he asked.

"Not much more than I told you over the phone this morning."

"So, what?"

"Born 1922 as Anton Livius in Tilsit. Grew up there. That's all we know about his early life. Presumably because the citizens' register was destroyed during the war."

"And later? When does he appear next?"

"1945, straight after the war. Basel customs at Riehen registered him as a fleeing German soldier. That wasn't unusual at the time. But then another few years pass without any trace of him, and that *is* unusual. Perhaps he went back to Germany. The next entry isn't until 1956. That's when he was granted citizenship in Rüegsbach in the Emmental."

"Why Rüegsbach? How did he end up there? And why did he change his name?"

"I don't know. It might be worth paying the place a visit."

Good idea, thought Hunkeler. A leisurely drive through the Emmental, up the Lueg hill, then down to the nearest restaurant for bratwurst and rösti. "When did he come to Basel?" he asked.

"1963. He lived on Dammerkirchstrasse. His allotment lease started in 1972."

"Was he single?"

"As far as I know."

"Strange," commented Hunkeler. "A burned-out German soldier who finds a new home in the Emmental and even adopts the local dialect, you'd think he'd want to stay in the Emmental. Unless something went seriously wrong."

"Yes, I'd say so."

"What's the situation with his Wehrmacht records? Can we not get hold of them? If he was a soldier, there should be some sort of documentation."

"I'm trying, but it's difficult. Many of those files were destroyed."

Hunkeler put a cigarette in his mouth but didn't light it. "Haven't you got an ashtray?" he asked.

"No. It's still on the table in the meeting room."

Hunkeler shoved the cigarette back in the box. "What are your thoughts, generally I mean?"

"It's hard to say," replied Lüdi. "I'm probably thinking the same as you."

"Which is?"

"Who would ram a meathook under another person's chin?" He quietly chuckled to himself, almost silently, and shook his head. "No, that's crazy. There must be a reason. Perhaps that reason is linked to Flückiger's past. Or what do you reckon?"

"Could be. Have a quick look who leases plot B26."

Lüdi reached for some papers on his desk. "Here. B26 is leased by Moritz Hänggi, address Gotthelfstrasse."

"Thank you, my angel."

When Hunkeler was taking the elevator down, he met Dr de Ville. "*Hélas*, Hünkelé," the doctor greeted him. "Why do those idiots have to get killed when we should be having a day off? Can't they show some consideration?"

"I share your sentiments. I would have preferred to stay in Alsace."

"*Elle pue, la merde.* It's a stinking pile of shit. I'm driving over to Dammerkirchstrasse. Do you want to come?"

Around 7 p.m., Hunkeler stepped through the doors of the Restaurant au Violon in the Lohnhof. The historic building was situated next to the old prison and had been his workplace for years. He loved the ornate windows of the Gothic church on the square and the old lime trees, now dripping in the rain. The view onto the city's rooftops, onto the Barfüsserkirche and the Minster. It was an oasis of calm. Recently, the Lohnhof had been converted into a hotel where guests could spend the night in a former cell.

Bardet was sitting in a window alcove that looked out onto the city. In front of him stood an empty bottle of 1999 Vouvray.

"Good drop?" asked Hunkeler.

"Heavenly," replied Bardet. "A dry Chenin blanc from the Loire. Fancy a glass?"

"No, I want to take a look at Flückiger's apartment."

"OK, I'll come with you."

They drove through the rain-drenched streets. For a long time, neither said a word. Then Hunkeler began with his confession.

"The third man in the allotment cabin was Detective Sergeant Madörin."

"*Non*," mumbled Bardet, shaking his head. "*Il est trop con. He is very stupid.*"

"I'm sorry, I can't undo what he did."

"That's scandalous. You know that, don't you?"

"Yes. If it gets out, we're done for. Here, he found this box in Flückiger's left-hand jacket pocket. It contains Viagra pills."

"So you want me to cover for you, *n'est-ce pas?*"

"What other option do I have? Take it, will you, for heaven's sake. Flückiger might still have been alive, you know. And anyway, there's nothing odd about an old man making use of a little something when he beds a woman."

Finally, Bardet took the box. "Over eighty and still horny," he remarked and almost laughed. "There's still hope for us then, *n'est-ce pas?* But what if they find traces of the drug in Flückiger's blood? How do we explain that?"

"Then we're in trouble."

"C'est une connerie, what a mess! It will cost you. A couple of dozen oysters, Fines de Claire. And several bottles of Vouvray."

The apartment was a two-bed, barely six hundred square feet, on the ground floor. The hallway was covered in plastic sheeting. Technicians were working in all the rooms. A table with two chairs in the kitchen, fitted shelves in the living room, a sofa and two armchairs complete with coffee table, no ashtray. The place looked uninhabited, like sparsely furnished holiday lodgings. The only thing that stood out were the red and white checked bedcovers.

"Found anything?" asked Hunkeler.

"Nothing worthwhile, no," replied de Ville. "Just passport, health insurance card, bank statements and so forth."

"How much has he got?"

"A few thousand francs. It looks like the guy didn't much like being here. Or he was hiding. There's no PC, just an old landline phone. No pictures on the walls, no photos. No box with letters. Just this." He pointed at the shelf next to the front door. It had a vase on it with faded paper flowers, and a miniature clog made of white porcelain with blue decorations.

"A souvenir from Holland, it would seem," commented de Ville. "It can be used as an ashtray."

"And the flowers?"

"They're the type you can win on fairground shooting stalls. These must be several decades old."

"Anything else?" asked Hunkeler. "Surely there must be something. He can't have lived without some memento or other."

"We found a few postcards without stamps, he never sent them. They were all in a yellow envelope. Here. From Amsterdam, Prague, Carlsbad, and one from Altkirch."

"Why Altkirch?"

"No idea. There's also one here from Sumiswald in the Emmental. It has some weird stuff written on it, like a secret language: Küssu, Köbu, Wäutu, Fridu, Ülu, Tönu. What do you make of that?"

"Mumbo jumbo. And the other cards, anything on them?"

"Yes, they all have writing on them. Here."

Hunkeler took the cards and looked at them. Pictures of a waterway in Amsterdam, the Charles Bridge in Prague, spa gardens in Carlsbad and the Zum Kreuz restaurant in Sumiswald. All of them tattered and discoloured. The writing on the back was faded, some of the letters in old German script.

"Where was this envelope?"

"In the kitchen, in the drawer under the table."

"OK. We'll deal with these postcards at the briefing tomorrow. Please see to it that the writing is made legible. Get an expert to take a look. Anything else?"

"Yes. There's a twelve-digit phone number noted on the yellow envelope. The dialling code is 006676, with the letters AK written in front. The code is for Phuket in Thailand. I don't know what the letters signify."

"You didn't call the number, did you?" Commissaire Bardet asked.

"*Mais non*, of course not. We don't meddle in other people's affairs."

"OK," said Hunkeler, "let's go and eat." He took Bardet by the arm and they left. "I don't like all that rummaging around," he said when they were back in the car. "A person's entire life is dragged out into the open, the most intimate details, nothing is sacred. It makes me sick. I know it has to be done. But that doesn't mean I have to be there when they do it."

"Let's head back to the Violon," suggested Bardet.

They started with oysters and wine. Commissaire Bardet fully devoted himself to his favourite pastime, drinking one glass after the other. In between, he quickly slurped three oysters and chewed them before he swallowed.

"Heavenly," Hunkeler remarked.

"Divine," Bardet agreed. "*C'est une merveille*, just marvellous." He picked up more oysters, which he slurped down with astounding speed, then ordered another two dozen.

Hunkeler gamely kept up. He hardly ever ate oysters, unless he was at the seaside. Now they conjured up memories of the salty wind on his face, the sharp smell of the Atlantic. He guzzled the white wine with pleasure and was impressed when Bardet ordered a third bottle.

The host placed a brown terrine of tripe on the table. It came with a bitter leaf salad. They chomped in silence, nodding at each other appreciatively. After the cheeseboard with the melting Camembert – it stank but tasted good – they settled down to business.

"How can a Basel prosecutor talk such utter rubbish?" Bardet asked as he lit a black Caporal cigarette. "Suter is a perfectly intelligent man, is he not? Would you like one?"

"Please," replied Hunkeler. "I used to smoke this brand. In Paris, back in the good old days." He got a light off Bardet and pulled the smoke deep into his lungs, instantly feeling a bit light-headed. "You don't do things by halves, do you?" he observed. "Eating, drinking, smoking. No complaints?" he asked Bardet.

"None as far as I'm concerned. But my wife complains that I'm too heavy for her. What can you do? I enjoy the good things in life, *c'est tout.*"

"Basel was once a free imperial city, of significance within Europe," Hunkeler said. "An ecumenical council was held here in the fifteenth century and Switzerland's first university was also founded here. It has always been a worldly city. It used to have several subject territories, but they were never that important for Basel, not like they were for Bern, for example. Basel made its money from printing, from science and trade, and more recently from the chemical industry. Basel society has always been a little aloof, a bit conceited perhaps, but also dynamic and smart. There's still a lot of money in this city. But it isn't brandished about, or at least only in the form of art. The art isn't made here, it's commissioned and bought in. Basel people are hunters and collectors. First they hunt for the money, then they collect art. Have you ever been in the Museum of Art?"

"Yes," replied Bardet as he sipped on a small black coffee. "Amazing what they have hanging in there."

"In 1833, Basel was stripped of the last subject territory it still had, the Baselland. Even today, Baselers still feel offended. They've been stewing in their own juices ever since. They no longer know how to talk to people from outside Basel, from Aargau or Alsace. Secretly, they still think they're the lords and the others are their loyal subjects. That's why Suter was talking such gibberish."

"And Madörin?"

"He's an overzealous pleb. He can be very tenacious, almost fanatical. Once he's got the bit between his teeth he doesn't give up until he's done what he's set out to do."

Bardet had ordered an Armagnac, in a brandy glass. He lifted it to his nose, sniffed, closed his eyes and drank. "*Merveilleux*," he commented. "Such exquisite aroma and taste. And what about you?"

"Is this some kind of interrogation?"

"Why not? I want to know who I'm working with."

"I'm a country boy. A bit rough around the edges, as you can see. From the much-belittled Aargau canton. I don't care, I like being from Aargau."

"*Douce France*," said Bardet, "*pays de mon enfance*. I'm Alsatian, from Blotze."

"I know it. There's a good inn there."

"Everywhere in Alsace has a good inn," replied Bardet and tipped the last drops of Armagnac into his mouth. "Will you have one too?"

"I still have to drive."

Bardet ordered another. He was nearly six and a half feet tall and evidently had no trouble holding his drink.

"Anton Flückiger also drank Armagnac," Hunkeler remarked. "In a brandy glass, just like you. In the Luzernerring. Mara told me, she's a waitress there."

"Odd," reflected Bardet, dreamily closing his eyes. "This brandy from Gascony is more refined than any cognac. Monsieur Flückiger should have drunk cognac and left the Armagnac for us." He was lost in thought for a while, then he continued. "I heard that during the Second World War, not a single drop of Armagnac could be found in all of France. The gentlemen of the Wehrmacht confiscated it all and drank it themselves. I guess they weren't all complete idiots, there must have been some connoisseurs too. At least they didn't destroy Paris. Or Colmar or Kaysersberg. *Oms Gottswille nid.* Heaven forbid. But they should have left us the Armagnac." He finished his second one, smacked his lips again and set the empty glass down on the table. "Why did Anton Flückiger drink Armagnac?" he asked. "How did he come to get a taste for it? Could it be that he was in France with the Wehrmacht? How come there's a postcard from Altkirch in his collection? Was he stationed in southern Alsace?"

Let him speculate, thought Hunkeler, he's heading in the right direction.

"It's perfectly possible, don't you think?" Bardet continued. "It's even possible that this potential fact has something to do with his murder."

"Yes, it's possible," replied Hunkeler.

"But it's also possible that this potential fact has nothing to do with the murder at all. That we should look for the perpetrator in the allotment community. Then again, the perpetrator might have known the victim through an entirely different channel. That means we have to adopt a multipronged approach. In any case, we urgently need access to Flückiger's military records."

"That appears to be difficult. We've been trying too."

"Have you? Did Detective Sergeant Madörin try?"

"No, Corporal Lüdi. Normally, these records are easily accessible. With Flückiger's file, that doesn't seem to be the case."

"What will happen with the postcards and the flowers?" asked Bardet.

"They'll all be handed over to the Police Nationale. As will all other information. We'll make copies, of course. After all, we're working together."

"OK. What about Madörin?"

"We'll let him loose on the allotment holders. He can ask around. He's good at that."

"If you like. As long as he keeps out of my sight." He reflected for a while. Then he smiled in an utterly disarming manner. "Did you not notice? The problem with the Viagra has resolved itself."

No, Hunkeler hadn't noticed.

"In the bathroom. The same box was lying on the shelf under the mirror. I've been wondering all this time whether Flückiger was a sex maniac."

"No, just a ladies' man," Hunkeler told him.

"Oh? What's the difference?"

"No idea."

Bardet grinned. He lit another cigarette. "Seeing as we trust each other, I will tell you. We've found something very strange. In the cabin, under the ground. One of the thick floorboards had a screw in it that had recently been loosened and screwed back in again. It was barely noticeable, someone had swept dirt over it. But one of our technicians still spotted it. We removed the board and found a recess underneath. In it was a large tin box. It was empty. Or nearly empty. There was some blood in it. Just a tiny amount, a few drops. So the question now is, what kind of blood is it."

"Blood in the cellar," commented Hunkeler. "A skeleton in the closet. I wonder what it's all about."

Bardet ordered another coffee, without sugar. "That's what we're wondering too. I've never heard of anything similar. A shot in the forehead, OK. A meathook under the chin, that's conceivable. But both together? And to then hang the victim up? One thing is clear, though. He was dead when he was strung up. There was certainly no fight, no life-and-death struggle."

"No? So what kind of struggle was it? The bed seemed to have been tipped over. And a chair too."

Bardet glanced up and shot him a surprisingly sharp look. "Anything else?"

"Yes. Madörin mentioned tracks. Two tracks that came from B26 and led to the exit. A man and a child. Or a man and a woman."

"It was a woman, according to our specialist. The man's tracks were barely identifiable. Several other people had walked along there. And the ambulance also drove across the path. *C'est vraiement une connerie.* It's a real mess." He sipped his coffee without enthusiasm now, as though he found it repulsive. "It stopped snowing at 3.42 a.m.," he said. "So the people from B26 must have left their plot after 3.42. Perhaps we should take a closer look at their cabin sometime." He pulled a piece of paper out of his pocket and looked at it. "B26 is being leased by a Moritz Hänggi. His partner is called Jeanette Wiest. That's a southern Alsace name. The couple boarded a flight to Fuerteventura at 1.50 p.m. today, departing from the EuroAirport. They're away for a week. Which is understandable in this weather." He was fed up. He also seemed to have the hiccups and was trying to suppress it.

"A few drops of blood, two tracks in the snow, and the Armagnac," said Hunkeler.

"Yes, not much to go on, dammit. Plus a few washed-out tracks that lead through the rear part of the allotments, across the field to Hegenheim."

When Hunkeler drove back into Alsace after 10 p.m., both border posts were manned. The Swiss guard knew him, he waved him through. The French one wanted to see his passport. "Have you had anything to drink?"

"No."

"Aha, a gendarme. They hung a guy up over there." The guard pointed across into the allotments, where the glare of the floodlights could be seen.

"I know. But I'm not currently on duty."

"Aha. Where are you off to?"

"To my house, near Folgensbourg."

"Aha, a neighbour, I live in Ranspach-le-Haut. Safe journey."

In Hegenheim, the Christmas decorations along the street were alight, among them a star of Bethlehem. How nice, thought Hunkeler, it's leading me to my stable.

Up on the ridge, there was still snow on the ground. He rolled along slowly, in second gear. There was hardly any traffic, the road was too treacherous.

The badger was gone. Someone must have lugged him into their car. You could see the drag marks, the red sheen in the snow where the animal had bled from its nose and mouth.

An unfamiliar car with a Basel plate was parked outside his house. Hunkeler walked up to the living room window and looked in. Two women sat at the table, a bottle of wine between them, bathed in the light from the lamp with the porcelain shade. What a cosy scene, he thought. What a lovely pair. He watched them, spellbound.

The visitor was Annette, Hedwig's friend and colleague from the kindergarten. She came from a stinking rich Basel family and seemed to have difficulty coping with her wealth on an emotional level. That was why she was very socially minded. Which was fine with Hunkeler. Essentially, he was too.

"You could have rung," said Hedwig when he came in. "We would have waited with dinner."

"Yes, I'm sorry. I keep forgetting I have a phone on me. I've already eaten, with a commissaire from Mulhouse."

"Seems to be an ugly affair. We heard about it on the radio."

"And? What did they say?"

"That an old man nearly had his head torn off."

"I don't know about that," said Hunkeler and poured himself a glass of red wine. "I don't know much at all, in fact. It could turn out to be a protracted business."

"You never have time. Not even over New Year."

"Oh, but I do, I'll take the time. Time is the only thing that helps me. I suggest we go for a walk tomorrow, after breakfast, come rain, snow or sleet. The three of us."

They clinked their glasses to that.

"What do people mean when they say someone's a ladies' man?" he asked.

Hedwig giggled, and Annette joined in. "Take a look in the mirror sometime, then you'll know."

"Nonsense," he said. "I'm as harmless as they come."

"What kind of folk are they, the allotment lot?" Annette asked him. "I mean in terms of social standing."

"I don't know. They seem to be an ordinary lot."

"Wasn't there a report of some kind, years ago, that caused a big stir? About a caravan park on the Rhine. It was by a well-known Zurich journalist. Or was he an author?"

"Niklaus Meienberg was his name," Hunkeler replied. "He was both, journalist and author."

"Yes. He really criticized that community, gave them a real roasting."

"Meienberg gave everyone a roasting."

"I don't see why those people shouldn't have their slice of happiness. In any case, I think it's good that the Basel authorities make that land available."

"I think it's good too. But none of us would last a single day in one of those allotments. Everything there is governed by strict rules. Apparently, that's necessary to prevent disputes. But then the rules themselves cause dispute. For example, the trunk of a fruit tree must be no more than fifty inches high. If your tree grows above this limit, you have to fell it."

"That makes sense," commented Annette. "Imagine someone plants a pear tree, and it grows and grows and its branches extend into the neighbouring gardens. Next thing you know, the neighbour comes with the axe and chops the tree down. And perhaps he also sinks the axe into the tree owner's head."

"That's what I mean," said Hunkeler. "It's intolerable."

He went to bed early that evening. He got into Hedwig's bed in the adjoining room and left the door open a crack, so he'd be able to hear the two women talking. They whispered, they giggled, they opened another bottle. He could feel the cat snuggling up against the backs of his knees. Then he fell asleep.

The next morning they ate an abundant breakfast. He'd let the hens out and had returned to the kitchen with three eggs. He made the fire, brewed tea and coffee, fed the cats. The usual morning chores, done slowly and carefully whenever he had time. And he had time.

When he was done, he went to wake the two women. Hedwig was lying on her stomach and snoring gently, as she always did when she was fast asleep. He kissed the nape of her neck.

"What is it?" she whispered.

"Time to get up, it's Bärzeli's Day. We're going for a walk, in honour of the holy St Berchtold."

"Who's he?"

"No idea. Breakfast is ready."

Annette padded down the stairs like a sleepwalker. Her hair hung down over her red dressing gown, and Hunkeler saw her hidden beauty. He loved that, sleepy-eyed women in the morning.

It was shortly after nine when they set off. The two trotted along behind him, in yellow plastic capes and rubber boots. The path was covered in slushy snow. It was still raining, but snowflakes drifted down amid the rain. The brook by the bend in the path had burst its banks, they waded on through.

When they reached the woods, Hedwig hooked her arm into his. "You're crazy," she said, "going for a walk in this lousy weather. You're so crazy it's contagious. And that's all right with me."

*

When Hunkeler drove back to Basel he took the route through the villages. He had a cosy sort of feeling. He went through Knoeringue, past the half-timbered houses with smoke rising from the chimneys, the Gothic church, and the Scholler restaurant beside it. Then the forest, pristine, untouched for a thousand years. No conifers, just oaks, beeches and acacias. It wasn't worth cultivating this woodland, the trees grew too slowly, were too gnarled.

He passed the Täufer farm up on the hill. The dairy cows were standing outside in the snow, black and white piebalds, more than forty of them. He saw the white water tower over Folgensbourg, and the Adler inn, where the mail coaches used to change horses. Then the gently sloping road down onto the plain. The EuroAirport on the left, and straight ahead the city of Basel with its dark church towers and the pale high-rises of the chemical industry.

The border posts were still manned. The usual idiocy, just plain annoying. As if the perpetrator could be caught here.

The Swiss border guard stopped him with a raised finger. Hunkeler's lyrical mood evaporated in an instant. "What is it?" he snarled. "What are you doing?"

"Passport, please. And nice and politely, please." Blank-faced, the guard leafed through the passport from front to back, then from back to front. "Is that right? Are you really an inspector?"

"Well, what do you think I'm doing here? Going out for a spin?"

"Apologies, but there's all manner of riff-raff milling around here. It's complete mayhem over in the allotments."

"Why, what's going on there?"

"Someone killed Beat Pfister's ducks. Must have happened last night. Despite the fact that nobody is allowed in unless they have animals. I know Beat. He would never kill his own ducks."

"Goddammit," Hunkeler grumbled.

He parked in front of the Blume. The lights in the command vehicle across the border were on and he could hear a compressor running in the allotments. Haller stood by the entrance, next to a gendarme. They were both laughing, probably telling each other jokes.

"How was it possible?" asked Hunkeler. "How could that happen?"

Haller put on his sad face. "I don't know. I'm not here during the night."

"So who is then?"

"Kaelin, with two colleagues. It happened on plot B76. That's right by the Golan."

"By the what?"

"Plot B76 is right on the edge of the allotments. There's a gravel mound there. The people call it the Golan Heights, because you can see into Alsace from it."

"They're all mad," shouted Hunkeler. "Who's in charge here anyway?"

Haller tapped out his pipe in an almost solemn manner. "You already know that."

"So what is this, an eye for an eye, a tooth for a tooth? And why are you constantly tapping that pipe?"

Startled, Haller shoved it in his jacket pocket. "What's up with you all of a sudden, Hunki?"

But Hunkeler wasn't listening, he was already walking back to the car. He got in, reached for the phone and called Bardet. He got voicemail. He called Lüdi. Voicemail again. He threw the phone onto the floor in front of the passenger seat.

What was the matter? Why was he suddenly so angry? Was it his age, were his nerves shot? Was he overtired? No, he'd had enough sleep.

He sat up properly, with his back long and straight, as far as that was possible in his small car. He placed his hands on his knees and tried to breathe slowly and smoothly. I'm feeling calm and relaxed, he said to himself, and my limbs are heavy and warm.

It was no good. He lit a cigarette. There, that was better.

So there was a feud going on in the allotments. Ruthless, merciless, to the bitter end. A few drops of blood in the cellar. Yesterday the rabbits, today the ducks, perhaps tomorrow one of the cabins would be on fire. And, for a bit of variety, a guy is hung up on a beam. It was like some kind of blood feud, like in the Balkans.

He was fed up. He didn't want to get involved in the dreary mess of it all. He knew there was nothing as relentless as the revenge of a petit bourgeois who'd been hurt in his pride. No, he was going to keep well away from this guerrilla war. Madörin could take care of it. He knew all about this kind of stuff, he had that same kind of petty mentality.

Hunkeler threw his cigarette out of the window and picked up the phone. Luckily, it was a robust make.

He went into the Blume. A delicious smell of roast meat hung in the air, the place was packed with people eating. Bottles of wine stood here and there, the Merlot from the tap had been replaced with a nice Beaujolais Villages. The mood was festive, like at a lavish funeral.

Among the group at the regulars' table were Martin Füglistaller and Jürg Stebler. They had made moves to stand up as soon as they saw him come in, but Siegrist held them back. Now they sat there like schoolboys caught red-handed.

Hunkeler was so surprised he stood rooted to the spot. He saw the man in the purple jacket, his Borsalino on the table in front of him. Opposite him sat a small, pug-faced woman. He saw Madörin in the corner at the back, together with contact man Morath and grounds warden Widmer. They all had a juicy slice of beef fillet in front of them.

He went over to Madörin's table. Nobody said a word. "Slept it off?" he asked.

"Yes, of course. I'm here for work."

"Business before pleasure, isn't that what they say? What are you doing here, Monsieur Morath?"

"We questioned Füglistaller and Stebler, over in the association's office," Morath replied. "We've put everything on record, it's all above board. The two clearly have nothing to do with the murder. Why shouldn't we join them for a meal?"

"Indeed, why not," said Hunkeler. He went to the regulars' table, grabbed an empty chair, reached for a glass and poured himself some wine. "Cheers, gentlemen."

Still nobody said a word. Then Siegrist took hold of his glass and lifted it to make a toast. "Let's raise our glasses to our late friend Anton Flückiger. May his soul rest in peace."

These were the right words at the right time. They all raised their glasses and drank.

"First the vigil by the body, then a funeral meal, it's only right and proper," said Hunkeler. "Can I have a slice of that fillet too? It looks good."

"Already on its way," replied Siegrist. "There's plenty for everyone."

And indeed the landlady then appeared with a plate. The meat was cooked medium rare, not too much and not too little, just right. It tasted fabulous. Hunkeler ate slowly, he needed time to think.

"It's an old allotment tradition," explained Siegrist. "We don't do it out at Hörnli cemetery, we do it here in the restaurant. Everyone's invited. Only the wine has to be paid for."

"A nice tradition," said Hunkeler. "And everyone has come to say farewell."

"All the regulars, that's true."

"Beef as well-aged as this is usually only available in Alsace," Hunkeler observed. "How much was it? Nine pounds? Ten?" He was champing away noisily now, then took a swig of his wine. "Herr Füglistaller and Herr Stebler, you have my sympathies. First you go and hide. Understandable – it's not easy, being a witness in a murder case. But at least you didn't go into hiding, or get on the plane to Fuerteventura."

Stebler was seized by a coughing fit. Something must have gone down the wrong way. Füglistaller was considerably more relaxed. "We're not witnesses," he said. "I just saw him hanging there when I had to step outside in the morning. But our conscience is clear."

"Yes, I understand," Hunkeler replied in an extremely friendly manner. "But if you don't tell me the truth right now, I'll have you arrested. As suspects."

He had expected Madörin to leap up at this point and start yelling, but he stayed sitting, nice and quiet.

"We put everything down in our statement," said Füglistaller. "Everything we saw. Everything we know."

Hunkeler smiled sweetly. He picked up a toothpick. "So why did you disappear once the ambulance had arrived? Why didn't you wait for the gendarmerie?"

"We'd had a lot to drink, we were probably still over the limit. We wanted to drive home in our cars without being breathalysed."

"That's enough now!" shouted Hunkeler. "Talk, or I'll send for the patrol car."

The vibe in the room was decidedly uncomfortable now. Everyone had stopped eating.

"Go on then, talk," said Siegrist. "It's not a crime, after all." Füglistaller nodded. "It's not our fault. Toni used to trade meat. Not in a big way. But he did make a hundred francs here and there. Everyone knew that. His nickname was The Butcher."

"He would buy a load, say for example ten pounds of beef fillet over in Hegenheim, and bring it into the allotments," Stebler chimed in. "He'd come through the back entrance by the Golan. That's allowed, for personal consumption in the allotments. But then he'd bring the meat into Switzerland through the main entrance. That's not allowed. But there's never anyone there to check. He then sold it on a bit below the Swiss price and made a good profit on it. Meat is much cheaper in Alsace."

"We knew he'd been over there on New Year's Eve," said Füglistaller. "We also knew he stored the meat under his cabin floor. So we searched until we found it. And it would be such a shame not to eat it now."

"You're right there," said Hunkeler. "Did you include that in your statement too?"

"No."

"And why not?"

"Because nobody asked about it."

Hunkeler poked around between two teeth, where a remnant of meat was still caught. Madörin, that bastard, he just wanted to protect himself. And Morath was no use for anything. All he cared about was that the treaty with France was rigidly adhered to.

"One more question. What other things are stored in the allotments? Wine, cognac, champagne? What is hidden where, and why? How deep underground can such a stash be buried?"

"Digging down under the cabin is not allowed," said Siegrist. "A lily pond mustn't be more than three feet deep. And it mustn't be lined with concrete, it has to be lined with membrane."

"They're the rules," Pfeifer agreed. "But Toni did dig around a fair bit when he first got his plot. He brought in concrete in a moped trailer and transported loads of soil away."

"Just for the lily pond," said Siegrist.

"Even though it's not allowed?" asked Hunkeler.

"I was already on the committee then, although I wasn't chair yet," Siegrist replied. "We discussed it, we decided to turn a blind eye. Concrete or membrane, it makes no difference from the outside."

"How right you are," said Hunkeler. "And who killed the ducks last night?"

The atmosphere in the room instantly grew even more uncomfortable.

"We have our suspicions," Siegrist said after a while. "We did include them in our statements, with the required prudence, of course. Anything else?"

"Yes," replied Hunkeler. "Many thanks for the meal. And remember this: I'm going to give you all a good hiding."

He drove to Kannenfeld Park, he needed exercise. It had started to snow again, the temperature had dropped. Bloody westerly, he thought. That damned warm spell that had confounded everything. It was intolerable. First Arctic winter with temperatures below zero since the beginning of December. Then a balmy föhn wind or whatever the hell it was, throwing his system into disarray. It was too much, especially for an old inspector like him.

He parked on Burgfelderstrasse, pulled on his jacket and went into the park. It was a former cemetery and hadn't been built on out of respect for the bones in the ground. The dead protecting the living.

He set off at a trot. He did three rounds, not too fast, he took short steps, panting like a dog. He felt his heart beat in his chest, the sweat on his forehead. Humans are flight animals, he thought. Go, Hunkeler, go! Keep moving, otherwise the Grim Reaper will get you.

He went into Erkan Kaya's cafe by the park entrance. A few years ago, there had just been a kiosk here, selling sweets, newspapers and cigarettes. Then Erkan had started serving coffee at a lone bar table. Several more tables were added, and a year ago three glass walls complete with a roof. It was like sitting in an aquarium, only the other way round. He sat in the dry, while outside mothers with their brightly dressed children floated past amid the snow flurries.

He ordered coffee with cold milk and looked around for a newspaper. There were no papers, St Berchtold's Day was a bank holiday. He was glad of it. Otherwise he would have had to read ridiculous articles about a corpse on a meathook in which almost nothing was true.

He spotted a writer he knew. He was standing at the bar smoking, with an espresso in front of him. He liked the guy, he'd read a good book by him, decades ago. A novel about Kleinbasel, about bourgeois bigots, unkindness and poverty. He was a widely known author back then, now he wasn't doing so well.

"Why don't you come and join me?" said Hunkeler.

"Gladly," replied the author. "You've probably just come from the allotments."

"I have."

"It's quite something, the brutality," said the author. "They were all working-class people once. I wrote for them. Not that they read my books, but they knew me and liked me. Now they all drive middle-class cars. None of them is interested in my work any more. Their class awareness has gone down the pan. All they want is to defend their own property, with a meathook if necessary."

"So what do you drive?"

The author laughed. "You're right, a middle-class car. I also have middle-class sensibilities, even though I can't afford them. But what can you do? One has to adapt. Anyway, I spend half the year on a Greek island. The cost of living is still low there."

"How's the writing going?"

"Ach well, I'm an old fart. How am I supposed to come up with new ideas? A detective novel now and then, that

I can still do. Set among former working-class people who have turned bourgeois. I know all about the sadness and hate that festers in those people. They'd stop at nothing, inspiration permitting."

Outside, Cattaneo appeared through the driving snow, with a female figure close behind. They steered towards the cafe.

"This murder in the allotments," the author went on. "That would make for a good story. It would be the ideal vehicle for describing the criminal energy of the allotment holders. People who lease their little kingdom for a small amount of money and will defend it to the death. 'Murder in the allotments', that would be a great title, wouldn't you say?"

Cattaneo came in, followed by the woman. He sat down, she sat down too. He hadn't turned to look at her a single time. In fact he didn't seem to be looking at anything at all, as if nothing was of interest to him. He ordered two coffees.

"And what about you?" asked the author. "How are you doing?"

"I'll be retiring soon. And then I'm off to Alsace."

"Oh yes, you have that house there. It's kind of odd that nobody wants to live out their days in our lovely Basel, don't you think? Everyone who can, gets out of here."

"I think it's normal. Cities are for the young. So, this story, how would you tell it?"

"Probably as a love story. By which I mean a story about the disappointment of a love betrayed. In my opinion, the brutality of the act allows for no other explanation."

"What is that, a love betrayed? I've often heard the expression, but I've never understood what's meant by it. Either you're in love or you're not. Where does betrayal fit into that?"

The author grinned with an air of superiority. Presumably he'd already been thinking about this. Perhaps he had already started writing. "We don't live in paradise any more, Inspector, you should know that. Pure love isn't possible in this day and age. The loved person becomes a commodity, a possession. And possessions, as we know, are defended by any means available."

"Interesting," Hunkeler remarked. He looked across at Cattaneo, who hadn't exchanged a single word with the woman.

"That man over there, he's a good example," said the author. "His name is Ettore, he's from Lombardy. He had a fantastic wife, Lucia. She looked after him well, was always chatting and laughing. A typical bouncy Italian woman, everybody liked her."

"You know everyone round here, don't you?"

"No, not everyone. Just the regulars. That's what comes from living alone. I don't want to sit in front of the TV on my own every evening. The two of them were a great couple. Until she strayed. He realized and from then on refused to touch her. She pined away and a few years later, she died. That's what people round here say. Whether it's true, I don't know. But it's certainly a good story for a crime novel."

"And who would the seducer be?"

Again the author grinned. It seemed he already had the story all planned out in his head. "Let's assume it was Toni Flückiger. He certainly was a womanizer. And there would have been plenty of opportunities, they both had an allotment. This is how the story would go: Lucia sleeps with Toni. Ettore avenges the betrayal by neglecting Lucia. Lucia suffers, she reproaches herself and feels guilt-ridden. She wastes away, falls ill with cancer and dies. Now it's Ettore's turn to feel guilty. He blames himself for not having forgiven his wife, thereby driving her to her death. The guilt threatens to suffocate him. He tries to assuage this guilt by shooting Toni in the head."

"That's all very well," said Hunkeler. "But why does he hang up the body with a meathook?"

"Out of desperation. He knows this murder won't rescue him. It's like an addiction. He has to increase the dose, even though it won't help. I wouldn't be surprised if he'd disfigured Flückiger's corpse in an even more gruesome way. Perhaps he chopped off his penis, who knows?"

"Or he pumped it up with Viagra," suggested Hunkeler.

The author's eyes narrowed. They were observation slits through which he peered at the inspector as if from inside an armoured vehicle. "Why do you say that?"

"I'm just thinking along."

"That's exactly what I was looking for," the author remarked. "May I use this idea?"

"If it helps you, go ahead."

When Hunkeler entered his office in the Waaghof he saw a pile of papers sitting on his desk. He weighed it in his hand and estimated how many pages there were. Certainly more than a hundred. The briefing would start at 4 p.m. as always, in just over an hour. It was the usual, everyday idiocy. How was an inspector supposed to plough through more than a hundred pages in an hour?

He picked up the top sheet. It was a list of the allotment holders grouped by nationality.

Share of Swiss 434. Share of foreigners 260. Of which foreigners Italy 157. Foreigners Spain 19. Foreigners Balkan countries 24. Foreigners Germany 0. Foreigners Turkey 25. Foreigners Austria 2. Foreigners France 0. Foreigners other countries 33.

He felt uncomfortable, but he wasn't sure why. Was it because of the author, who had presumptuously reconstructed and even explained the crime based on his own fantasy? Who did those scribblers think they were? Did they think they were cleverer than the CID? Yes, imagination was necessary in his line of work. As was insight into human nature. And often it wasn't the explicable that provided the key to solving a cryptic case, but the inexplicable, entirely improbable, or even downright ludicrous. Hunkeler had seen it many a time. Someone who committed a murder, who therefore defied the fundamental taboo of humankind, also defied human rationality. Such a person couldn't be comprehended with common sense and reason.

Was that true? Or was it just some far-fetched theory? In any case, these lines of thought weren't important to him. Hunkeler didn't care much for theories, he preferred a more practical approach.

He picked up a bundle of sheets which detailed the allotment allocation. Cattaneo had C25, right next to B35.

Something didn't feel right. And noticing this, he now realized why he felt so uncomfortable. He had encountered two different Cattaneos. First the jovial, cheerful Cattaneo at the regulars' table who had introduced himself as his neighbour. Then the desolate, morose Cattaneo who didn't even seem to be aware of his immediate surroundings. Why did he claim to be in love? You could see straight away that he wasn't.

Why had he got together with another woman? Perhaps he needed someone to do the cooking, washing and ironing. A live-in maid, someone who was happy to be taken in. She had followed him around like a dog.

Perhaps the author wasn't so wrong with his story. Perhaps Cattaneo really had killed Toni Flückiger, in revenge for the betrayal. With that act, he had bid farewell to life and was now waiting for death.

Hunkeler decided to keep the idea in mind. He rang Bardet.

"*Oui?*"

"I have news, Monsieur Bardet. The problem with the blood has been resolved."

"I know. It's oxblood. But where from?"

"From ten pounds of superbly aged French beef fillet. Flückiger intended to smuggle the meat into Switzerland. Füglistaller and Stebler found it. We ate it today for lunch. It tasted fantastic."

"*Le salaud.* Bastard," commented Bardet. "So, we have one problem less. OK, see you at the briefing."

The entire Basel crew was present, including Madörin. The French party consisted of Madame Godet, Monsieur Bardet and Monsieur Morath. The mood was tense from the start, although Prosecutor Suter was trying to assume a nonchalant air. He'd gone for casual sporty attire. Light grey flannel suit, pale pink shirt, dark blue tie. He was probably still struggling to leave the snowy slopes of Grisons behind and fully arrive in his dreary everyday life in Basel.

He briefly welcomed everyone, without mentioning the nationality of those present, then handed over to Madame Godet. She declared herself happy with the way the collaboration had got under way. They were, she continued, not yet in a position to present any detailed results. Their inquiries were ongoing, they were expecting to receive the first findings from the autopsy tomorrow, Tuesday.

Bardet also kept it brief. He didn't seem entirely comfortable in the assembled group and spoke without his customary sharpness. Perhaps the Vouvray and oysters were still sitting heavily in his stomach.

He said he didn't want to venture into speculation. But he did have the following to say.

Point one, Anton Flückiger had weighed 130 pounds. A lightweight. Hence it was perfectly conceivable that a single, strong man could have hung up the corpse on his own.

Point two, Flückiger had been shot at close range, with no signs of resistance. They had found the bullet in the timber wall of a neighbouring cabin. The bullet was modern, but had been fired from an older gun. It was possible that the gun dated back to the Second World War.

Point three, they hadn't yet managed to determine Flückiger's military career, the reason for this being that today was a holiday and the relevant archives were closed.

Point four, plot B35 was only sparsely cultivated. A rose bush, a yew tree and a lily pond. The pond had been constructed with reinforced concrete. They were currently breaking up the concrete and digging deeper in the hope of making a relevant discovery. They were also digging over the entire plot, which was difficult as the ground was frozen.

Point five, the meathook had come from Füglistaller's cabin. They had found several more such hooks hanging there.

Point six, a new command post would be in operation by this evening, situated in the French custom house.

Point seven, would the Swiss please send someone to Rüegsbach to make enquiries about Flückiger being granted citizenship. He was thinking of Inspector Hunkeler.

Prosecutor Suter sniffled audibly at this point, as if a midge had flown up his nose. He evidently felt his authority was being compromised, but he didn't say anything.

Bardet continued. Point eight, they had called the phone number in Thailand, but hadn't been able to obtain any definite information. They had enquired with the Thai telecommunications agency. The information was confusing. It appeared that the holder of that number was some sort of combination of pharmacy and brothel. They had tried several times. Nobody there seemed to know an Anton Flückiger.

Point nine, it was worth noting that Moritz Hänggi, who leased B26, had flown to Fuerteventura yesterday lunchtime. There was proof that Hänggi had spent New Year's Eve in B26, which seemed odd so shortly before his flight. Several attempts had been made to call him. It always went straight to voicemail, with a message saying that the person they were ringing didn't want to be disturbed.

"Why Moritz Hänggi?" Suter asked.

"Because he is of interest to us."

"But why?"

"We will disclose that when we feel the time is right."

Suter raised his hand to his pink shirt collar, but still didn't say anything.

"We are running this investigation," said Bardet. "We're not obliged to inform you of all the details. Is that not so, Monsieur Morath?"

"Indeed," replied Morath. "According to the treaty, that is correct."

"Thank you. Dr de Ville will now inform you of the findings from the inspection of Flückiger's apartment on Dammerkirchstrasse. I apologize for not elaborating any further. That is all we know."

"Apart from B26," Madörin said pointedly. "Apart from what might have happened on plot B26." He sat there in a strangely crouched position, as if he was about to leap into the air.

Hunkeler lit a cigarette. He was glad Bardet still had the ashtray on the table in front of him.

For a while, nobody said a word. Then Suter reached for his phone and ordered a round of coffee from the cafeteria.

"And a cognac, please," added Bardet.

"I'm sorry, Monsieur," replied Suter in an overly friendly tone. "We don't have any cognac. But I brought a delicious schnapps back with me from Davos. I have the bottle in my office. I'd be happy to fetch you a glass if you urgently need it."

"Messieurs, please," Madame Godet interrupted. "What is this? We're not in a kindergarten. Surely you're not going to start throwing punches. Please don't forget that you are in the presence of a woman." She attempted another of her charming smiles. It came off brilliantly this time.

"*Mais non*, Madame, we're good neighbours," Suter assured her, his voice sweet as honey. "At least that's how we see it from our side."

The man from the cafeteria arrived with the coffee. They sat with their cups in front of them, stirring in sugar, sipping. At one point, Lüdi's chuckle could be heard. It sounded helpless.

"I would like to know what your plans are regarding B26," Madörin eventually said. "Why did you let Moritz Hänggi slip away and fly off to Fuerteventura? Together with Jeannette Wiest, his partner. She's Alsatian, which could be relevant. Furthermore, I'd like to know why you're showing such little interest in the allotment holders. The Swiss, former Yugoslavs and Turks. Have you not heard that four ducks were killed last night? Don't you know about the dead rabbits? Your approach seems very one-sided, Monsieur Bardet."

Bardet stubbed out his cigarette. He looked like he was close to walking out. "Right," he said, stone-faced. "I suggest Monsieur de Ville now fills us in on Flückiger's apartment."

"What's going on?" shouted Madörin. "Do I get a clear answer or not?"

"*Non*," Bardet replied.

Madörin hurled his chair aside and left the room without a word.

"*Mais messieurs*," Madame Godet pleaded. "Can we please talk to each other like civilized human beings? *Je vous en prie.*"

Suter ran a hand over his hair as if he needed to make sure it was still there. His face hadn't lost its tan. Lüdi chuckled again, almost inaudibly. Hunkeler had an urge to burst out laughing, but he restrained himself.

"National borders exist, whether we like it or not," de Ville eventually said. "And so does the international treaty. *Was isch de los, nom de Dieu?* What's the matter? Have you all gone mad? Come on now. So, the apartment contained barely any keepsakes or memorabilia. It's as if Anton Flückiger had tried to wipe away the traces of his life. Three paper flowers and a few postcards, that's all. The paper flowers, three roses which must have once been bright red, are the type you can win at funfair shooting stalls. You can still get them today in Alsace. Flückiger presumably shot them down for a woman. The postcards are from Amsterdam, Prague, Carlsbad, Altkirch, and Sumiswald in the Emmental. They weren't posted. All of them have a date written on the back, plus a list of male forenames. The writing is faded in parts. We've had it transcribed by a specialist. I suggest we look at them in chronological order." He switched on the projector. "On the left you have the original card, on the right the transcription. Please note the capital letters *AK* and *FW*. You will see more capitals as we go along. Please also take note of those."

Everyone read what was shown on the screen.

Amsterdam, 8 October 1940. AK. Hans FW, Friedbert, Werner, Eberhard, Alfred, Anton.

Prague, 8 April 1941. AK. Egon HM, Matthias, Thomas, Jürg, Pirmin, Dieter, Christoph, Anton.

Carlsbad, Christmas 1941. AK. Egon HM, Martin, Friedrich, Adolph, Anton.

Altkirch, Katharinenmarkt 1942. AK. Peter OF, Jürg, Robert, Rudi, Joseph, Viktor, Theo, Anton.

Sumiswald, Kalter Markt 1958. AK. Küssu, Köbu, Wäutu, Fridu, Ülu, Tönu.

"The Katharinenmarkt fair in Altkirch takes place at the end of November," de Ville added. "Does anyone know when the Kalter Markt fair in Sumiswald is held?"

"Always on 30 December," replied Hunkeler. "I know because I had a weekend cottage in that area for several years. The names are Markus, Jakob, Walter, Fritz, Uli and Anton."

"OK," said de Ville. "Presumably those are all names of people with whom Livius visited these places. The cards give us some idea of his movements through Europe during the early years of the war, up to the end of 1942, when he was in Altkirch. Then the trail goes cold, until he reappears in Riehen near Basel at the end of the war. I consider Sumiswald a mere addition."

"What does *AK* stand for?" Madame Godet asked.

"We don't know. *A* could stand for Armee, *K* Kommando. *FW* could mean Feldwebel, *HM* Hauptmann, *OF* Offizier. These are just assumptions."

"Wasn't there a military hospital in Carlsbad?" asked Madame Godet.

"Yes. That might mean Anton Livius suffered a war injury."

"Is it possible to glean any concrete information from the listed names?"

"No. For us, they are just random names."

"It's strange that Livius kept a postcard from Altkirch," Madame Godet commented. "It's such a dump. Other than that, I have no questions."

"The three paper flowers are also a bit odd," said Morath. "Why three? And why did the shooter who got them, presumably Livius, keep hold of them instead of giving them to the woman he won them for?"

Nobody had an answer to that.

"I believe we're simply being strung along here," said Bardet. "Young men shoot down those paper flowers to impress a girl. Nobody keeps something like that into their old age. And the postcards are more reminiscent of a school trip. Except that a schoolboy would send such cards home, or to his girlfriend. In my opinion, it isn't worth attaching too much importance to these mementos."

"It's all we have, at least so far," de Ville pointed out.

"True, it's possible that Livius aka Flückiger intentionally laid a false trail," said Lüdi. "But it's also possible that the paper flowers and postcards did mean a lot to him. Which would lead us to the question of why?"

"Go on," said de Ville.

"*AK* appears on each of the cards. *AK* could indeed stand for Armeekommando. But what would an army commando be doing in Sumiswald? The letters could also stand for Alte Kameraden, old comrades. That would mean Livius had a constant need to surround himself with companions, with friends. That he was very lonely, a drifter. It would also explain why he didn't post the cards and kept them instead."

"An interesting psychological profile," commented Suter. "And what would you say is the significance of the three paper flowers?"

"It's possible the paper flowers reminded him of a happy youth. There must be a reason why he kept them. Again, his rootlessness might have something to do with it. Three roses as a token of love from his early years."

"The waitress at the Luzernerring knew him quite well," said Hunkeler. "She told me she had regularly seen him write postcards in recent times. She doesn't know who to.

81

He didn't keep those cards, he posted them. We should find out who to. And what he wrote on them."

"Very interesting, very interesting indeed," said Suter. "How do you intend to find that out?"

"By driving to Rüegsbach."

Nobody had any objections to that.

"I'd like to add something regarding the token of love from his youth," said Bardet. "Attached to the wall of his cabin on B35 are a dozen photos from Thailand, all showing naked beauties. We know from the airport that Livius regularly flew to Thailand, at least twice a year. That doesn't fit with your theory."

"Why not?" Lüdi asked. "It wouldn't be the first time someone who was disappointed in love turned into a whoremonger."

"*Mais quelle horreur,*" exclaimed Madame Godet. "Please mind your language."

"Why didn't you tell us straight away?" asked Suter. "Why have you been keeping important information from us?"

"All in good time," replied Bardet. "We're under no obligation to tell you everything. We also found another postcard with *AK* on it in the cabin. It's from Phuket in Thailand. From an establishment called the Sunshine Inn. As far as we've heard, it was a cheap guest house with a brothel attached. In addition to Anton, the card is again signed by a Peter, a Jürg and a Robert. We have compared the signatures with those on the card from Altkirch. It's the same three men, they were just several decades older in Phuket. We've been told that Peter, Jürg and Robert were long-term guests at the Sunshine Inn. They lived there. Anton visited them regularly. It seems that the Sunshine Inn was washed into the sea by the Boxing Day tsunami. In any case, the three gentlemen were declared dead. Strangely, all three of them had Thai passports with English surnames."

Suter smacked the table with the flat of his hand. His angry red face was at odds with his suave pink shirt. "Why weren't we informed of this at the start?"

"To tell you the truth," said Bardet, "I'm bored sick of all this. Let the old codgers spend their twilight years where and with whom they want. Anything else?"

Nobody said a word.

"Thank you, Messieurs," continued Bardet. "Madame Godet and I will now get to work."

After the two had left, the group met in the cafeteria. Suter was visibly outraged over the wilful withholding of information, as he called it. But he managed to exercise restraint, as contact man Morath was also present. Madörin was there too, full of repressed anger. "What are we doing here, anyway?" he asked. "We're wasting our time. What do we care that Livius flew to Thailand? Let's face it, it wasn't any of the Thai whores who killed him."

"It's all in line with the international treaty," Morath piped up. "I can attest that everything has proceeded correctly so far."

"Let's get to the point, shall we?" said Suter. "My view is that the perpetrator is more likely to be found among the allotment users than in Thailand."

"Well, it's blindingly obvious that all hell has broken loose in the allotments," Madörin shouted. "It's pure hatred in there. Someone needs to take the trouble to go there. Talk to the people, get stuck in, dig the dirt. But that's too much like hard work for that fancy-pants from Mulhouse. You were there, Monsieur Morath, weren't you? You heard what the allotment holders told us."

"True," Morath agreed. "There's some sort of culture war going on in the allotments. In that respect, they reflect our society as a whole. Reminiscent of the burning cars in the suburbs of Paris."

What an idiot, thought Hunkeler, but he didn't say anything.

"If you'll allow me, I'll summarize what we've found out about the actual situation," Madörin continued. "It all started when some of the people from the Balkans and Turkey got into the habit of listening to music very loudly. And I mean their own kind of music. Belly dancing stuff or the devil knows what. In any case, not the kind of music that would be suitable for the allotments."

"What do you mean?" asked Lüdi. "What kind of music would you class as suitable?"

"I don't know," replied Madörin. "Music from round here, I suppose, Central European music. Requests from grounds warden Widmer to turn down the volume were ignored. Despite the fact that the allotment regulations clearly state that the warden's instructions must categorically be followed."

"Language issues also posed a problem," added Morath. "There are allotment holders from the Balkans who barely speak a word of German. This significantly hampers communication."

"A typical integration problem then," said Suter.

"Rubbish," argued Madörin. "The message to turn down the radio should be easy to convey. But some of those people are simply wilful. They don't want to understand.

"Then a few of them started to barbecue meat, the way they would back home. Mutton with a lot of garlic and herbs from their home countries. This caused unpleasant odours. Particularly affected by this were Messieurs Füglistaller, Stebler and Anton Flückiger. It was mainly Messieurs Ferati and Begovič from the Balkans who did the barbecuing. Ferati has C31, Begovič C29. In a westerly, those two plots are exactly upwind of B39, B37 and B35. That was simply too much for the three Swiss. Again, they lodged a complaint with grounds warden Widmer. He intervened, again without success.

"Also, the leaseholder of C35, a Turkish Kurd by the name of Dogan, has an eighteen-year-old daughter called Dilara. She attends college in Basel, but she wears a head covering and long-sleeved clothing. She often works in the allotment, wearing the headscarf even on the hottest summer days. She has planted a large herb garden. She's often visited by a young Turk called Fidan, who doesn't seem to understand a single word of German. Evidently, Dogan doesn't like this Fidan coming by. On several occasions, there have been proper clashes between the two – in their own language, of course. These Turkish shouting matches have created further annoyance.

"And then this Dogan turned up with a live lamb one day. He wanted to slaughter it on his plot. In response to the remonstrations from Füglistaller and Stebler he apparently replied that Füglistaller slaughters his rabbits on the plot too."

"That's correct, those are the four points we have detailed in our protocol," said Morath.

"I see, very interesting," said Suter. "But what has that got to do with Flückiger's murder?"

"It all started small," Madörin replied. "Then it gradually snowballed. We're not claiming that one of those three, meaning Ferati, Begovič or Dogan, is the perpetrator. But we shouldn't discount the possibility either. First, someone knocked over Ferati's barbecue and smashed it to pieces. Nobody's willing to comment on who might have done it. Ferati himself says he doesn't know."

"Did you talk to him?" Hunkeler asked.

"Yes, in his apartment on Murbacherstrasse. Füglistaller and Stebler told us that Anton Flückiger was suspected of it. That happened in early September. On 4 December Füglistaller's rabbits were killed. It's clear Ferati could be the culprit."

"Why is that clear?" asked Suter.

"Because it must have been an act of revenge. Why else would anyone kill harmless rabbits?"

"But Füglistaller isn't the one suspected of destroying the barbecue, it's Flückiger."

"It could have been Füglistaller who knocked down the barbecue," said Morath. "It could be that they're now simply laying the blame at Flückiger's door because he's dead and can't defend himself."

"Another act of revenge was then committed," Madörin went on. "Begovič's cabin was broken into in mid December. The radio and CD player were wrecked. In the same night, Dogan's cabin was also targeted. Islamic scripts were taken and torn up."

"For God's sake," exclaimed Suter. "I hope it wasn't the Koran. That would be a scandal. Why was none of this reported to the police?"

"Because the allotment holders don't want anything to do with the police," said Madörin. "They say they can sort things out themselves."

"And who is supposed to have killed Pfister's ducks?" asked Suter.

"We don't know. But certainly someone whose pride was deeply wounded. We will continue to investigate. We may need to take one or another of them into custody. Personally, I suspect the perpetrator is a foreigner. But we must keep an open mind. Theoretically, it could have been just about anyone who leases a plot in the community allotments. Also, we should definitely check out the Cannibal Frost lads by the adventure playground. They're always raging on about so-called bourgeois conformists. And allotments are seen as the pinnacle of conformism. What's clear is that we can't leave the investigation entirely in the hands of the Police Nationale. They're not up to it. It's on us, the Basel CID, to take charge here. And I am collaborating intensively with Monsieur Morath, who is always present."

Suter turned to Morath. "And what's your opinion on this?"

Morath thought for a while, he seemed a little uncomfortable. Finally, he nodded. "As long as I'm kept informed of everything, it should be OK," he said.

Hunkeler was sitting in the kitchen of his apartment on Mittlere Strasse. It was 8 p.m. on Monday evening, 2 January.

Out in the back courtyard the air was full of snow. It fell silently, without a breath of wind; winter had made a full comeback. He loved this peace, it was a snowy peace.

He heated up a pizza and drank a pot of black tea. He asked himself what he should do. It would be easy to give up, to keep a low profile, to sit tight and wait. Wait until the case resolved itself of its own accord or simply fizzled out as the investigative machinery gradually slackened. Nobody would notice, it was a time-honoured practice among civil servants. And anyway, he was only officially required for special tasks now. Which meant he was generally left in peace.

But he didn't want to be.

He certainly didn't believe in the old comrades' Thailand connection, if indeed they were old comrades. His gut instinct told him that. Nor did he believe in the culture war. His brain told him that. He believed in what the waitress Mara had told him. She had liked Flückiger, perhaps even loved him.

He called Hedwig.

"Yes? When will you be getting back?"

"It's going to be late, but I'd like to sleep in with you tonight," he said.

"As long as you don't wake me up, that's fine. We've decided, Annette and I, to drive to Colmar for a few days. To visit the Isenheim Altarpiece and the *Madonna of the Rose Garden*. It's so peaceful outside. With the snow falling all soft and silent. That's what gave us the idea. Will you come with us?"

"Yes, I'll come. But only once the case has been solved."

"Oh, we can forget about that then," she replied.

"No. Anyway, who's going to look after the hens?"

"You're the farmer, not me."

"I'm not a farmer, for God's sake. I'm a poor, harried hunting dog. I have to drive to the Emmental tomorrow."

"Tough luck. But tonight you're coming here?"

"Yes, I already said I would."

"Your neighbours will look after the hens, if you don't want to. The farmer's wife will gladly have the eggs."

He drove to the Luzernerring, went into the bar and sat down at a table on the right.

"Can you spare me a minute?" he asked when Mara brought his coffee.

She ran her fingers through her hair and looked across to the regulars' table, where three men sat in silence. "Yes, happy to."

"Did Flückiger have any signs of an injury? I mean, did he have a scar?"

"Isn't that quite an intimate question?"

He didn't reply.

"OK then. He had a long scar across his belly button. It wasn't nice to look at, it must have been stitched together in a makeshift way. He spoke about it once. A shot to the stomach, in Bohemia. He nearly died from it. He was nursed in a hospital in Carlsbad." She reflected for a while, as if she was recalling her youth. He wanted to say something, but didn't know how. "He wasn't a bad person. Something haunted him, something he couldn't talk about. He survived being shot in the stomach. But he had a deeper wound some-where, one that hadn't healed. Once, he said he wondered why he was still alive. Why he had grown old while others had to die young." She ran her fingers through her hair again and blushed as she did it, like a girl after her first kiss. "I've never known a man who could give himself so fully to a woman," she said. "He completely surrendered himself, as if he could find salvation in this surrendering. I don't know how else to put it."

Hunkeler nodded. He understood.

"He was so incredibly kind. We liked consoling him. We women, I mean. Does it help you, what I'm saying?"

He nodded again. He wanted to know more. "Is it possible that one of these women had anything to do with his murder?" he asked.

"Do you mean, was it a woman who killed him? No, never. On the contrary, we looked after him."

"Do you know he travelled to Thailand?"

"Of course I know. Is that supposed to be a bad thing? The women there need to earn a living too." Looking across to the regulars' table, she hesitated. Then she said it anyway. "I lied to you yesterday. I know where he sent the postcards. To Thailand. He had friends there."

"Did he? And did those friends write back?"

"Yes. But not to his address on Dammerkirchstrasse. They were sent here, to the Luzernerring. Letters, in an envelope. He read them and immediately tore them up. He threw them in the wastepaper basket behind the bar. I had a look once, to see what was in them. There was a capital *A* and a capital *K*. And below it three names."

"What names?"

"Peter, Robert, Jürg. Nothing else. Apart from three flowers."

"Pardon?"

"Someone had drawn three flowers on the paper. It looked like three roses."

"Goddammit," Hunkeler said so harshly it made Mara jump.

"Have I said something wrong?"

"No, no, it's fine. I just need to think. Why three roses? Do you have any idea?"

"No, not really. Perhaps because roses are a symbol of beauty. Three roses, that means health, happiness and peace. That's what he was looking for all his life. I think he found it with me, for a few moments at least. That was why I loved him."

A proud, self-assured woman, Hunkeler thought. She knew what she was talking about. "Is there a woman here in Basel he was especially fond of? Apart from you, of course?" he asked her.

The question didn't bother her. She smiled amiably. "Lucia. She was a fantastic woman. She's dead now, of course."

"What did Cattaneo have to say about it?"

"*Ach, he.* He's such a bully, he didn't deserve Lucia. He was terribly jealous. Even though all he'd ever done was insult her."

"Do you know which bar Cattaneo frequents?"

"Have a look in the Milchhüsli. After the late-night news."

Hunkeler drove along Burgfelderstrasse towards the city centre. The snow was falling so heavily, he had to set the wipers to fast. A line 3 tram came towards him, he nearly didn't spot it. On the left was Kannenfeld Park. The tree branches lay draped across the fence, weighed down by the snow. Erkan's cafe was all dark, shrouded in a soft night glow.

Odd, he thought, how Mara had talked to him. She had revealed everything she could. Why had she done that? Because she loved Anton Flückiger. She loved him, even though she hadn't been his only woman.

A gentle wistfulness crept over Hunkeler as he thought of this. He felt a hint of envy. Then he grinned. He had enough to do with Hedwig. And he certainly couldn't tolerate having to share Hedwig with another man.

Also, Mara wouldn't have disclosed her secret to just any police officer. She had told him, nobody else. That made him happy.

He parked in front of the Milchhüsli. He saw the outlines of some guys sitting in the billiards hall across the road. It had large windows as it had been a co-op once. He wouldn't be going back in there for a while. He was angry at the landlord, who was from Albania. He had told him Switzerland was a broken country. No, Hunkeler had replied, it's Albania that's broken, not Switzerland. The man then claimed he was allowed to have several wives. But not in Switzerland, Hunkeler had pointed out.

He entered the Milchhüsli and sat down at the bar. Milena, the Serbian landlady, went to fetch him a beer, but he asked for a mineral water. He still had to drive.

"In this weather?"

"Yes," he replied, "over to Alsace, to my girlfriend. She's waiting for me." Young men were playing billiards in the side room at the back. Calm and focused, they pursued their game. With no work to go to, they would carry on playing until three in the morning. He saw the unemployed gardener sitting by the window to the right. Hunkeler liked him, he was from the Aargau too. But now wasn't the time.

Hunkeler pictured a young man who had become a soldier in early life. Livius wasn't yet twenty when he was sent to the Netherlands with the Wehrmacht. Then off to Prague, and no choice in the matter. In Bohemia he was shot in the stomach, perhaps by partisans. Then, for the first time in his young life, he was lucky, he survived. Onwards to Altkirch, right outside Basel.

Hunkeler had been four at the time, playing in the garden with snail shells. Anton Livius, or whatever his real name was, had suffered an emotional injury in Alsace which, according to Mara, weighed on him more heavily than the physical wound. After the war, he drifted around unregistered, perhaps in Bohemia or the devil knew where. Then he settled in the Emmental, was granted citizenship and took on a new name. Until he came to Basel aged forty and then, as an old man, was hung up with a meathook. But right until the end, he'd stayed in touch with his old pals, some of whom had moved to Thailand, and sent them postcards. And right until the end, he had sought solace in women.

Was that true? Had he really found solace? According to Mara, yes.

Hunkeler thought of his own, modest life. His trips to Paris, to the Quartier latin, in his younger years. He'd thought of himself as a wild guy, nonconformist and autonomous. He'd know a few women over the years. He'd married and they'd had a daughter. Then he got divorced. He was an officer in Basel's police service, an inspector with a good reputation, known for his sound investigative instinct. Now he had a girlfriend whom he loved and was waiting for his retirement, which he intended to spend in Alsace until he died.

Truly a modest life. Well, what could you say, he was a spoiled Swiss citizen.

At 10.30 p.m. Beat Pfister came in and sat down next to him at the bar. They ordered a half-bottle of Beaujolais, to share. Pfister was very agitated. He couldn't stay sitting on the stool, he had to stand up. "Who could be so cruel to four harmless ducks?" he whined. "Wringing their necks. Not to cook and eat them. No, they were just dumped outside my cabin. Who would do this to a respectable, blameless pensioner? I treasured those creatures above all else. They were always happy when I arrived in the mornings. They ate out of my hand. They nipped me in the arm, but never so hard it hurt. How can anyone even think of doing something like that? What kind of people are they?"

"Yes, what's your opinion?" Hunkeler asked him. "Who could have done it?"

"Well, you don't need to search far. But we'll smoke them out. If the police don't do it, we will. Nothing is sacred to those Muslims. Not their own wife, not their own daughter, not creation itself. They declare themselves lord and master over all around. They want to rule the world, even here in Switzerland. We took them in, we were kind to them and gave them food. Just imagine what it will be like if they go building their minarets all over the place. All that yelling from loudspeakers every few hours. Those Arabic *surahs* they want to shout into our ears. I was in Marrakesh for a few days in October. It was unbearable, all that racket. My wife went to pieces over it. Thank goodness we had earplugs with us. But the Swiss people won't allow an imam to rule over Basel. We have our Minster bells. And we're going to keep them."

"Don't worry," said Hunkeler. "I'm sure nobody's going to take away our Minster bells."

"Not yet," shouted Pfister, "but soon. In a few decades there will be no real Swiss children any more. There will only be little Mohammedans. Then we'll be in trouble."

"Well, if that's the case, perhaps you should have another stab at it yourself. What do you reckon?" Hunkeler suggested.

Pfister tried to think what Hunkeler might have meant by this. He couldn't work it out. "How do you mean?" he asked.

Hunkeler turned to Milena. "Does Cattaneo not come here any more?"

"No," replied Milena. "Not for the past three days. He wasn't even in here on New Year's Eve before he went to his allotment. Nor yesterday."

"Does he usually come with his new woman?"

"No, he comes alone."

"And what does he drink?"

Milena hesitated. "Do I have to tell you that?"

"You don't have to. But you can if you want to help me."

"Well, all right then. We have a cheap red wine from Serbia. You wouldn't want a single drop of it, it's so sour. He drinks a bottle and a half of it. He goes home around two. He says he can't sleep without the wine."

"So what does he do now?"

"No idea. I've been worried about him. He's been acting so strange recently."

"Strange in what way?"

"You're looking for Toni Flückiger's murderer, aren't you?"

Hunkeler nodded.

"He would change from one minute to the next, it was like flipping a switch. It would happen really fast. First he'd be talking and laughing, then suddenly he'd go mute as a fish. As if he wasn't even aware of the world around him any more. As if some kind of inner image had shifted in front of his eyes. Do you know what I mean?"

"Yes, possibly."

"I don't know if it was because of his dead wife, perhaps that's what was haunting him."

"Lucia."

"Yes. Did you know her?"

"No, unfortunately not."

"From one second to the next his face would go pale and he'd go limp, an old man. If I said something to him, he didn't seem to hear. He would sit there like that until he'd finished his wine and paid."

"But he has a new partner, doesn't he?"

"Yes, Giovanna. But she's only with him because she has nowhere else to go. Are you sure you want to drive to Alsace tonight?"

"Yes, of course. Good night."

He went outside, got in his car and set off. He drove all the way in second gear. The French border post was manned by the officer from Ranspach.

"Do you think I'll get through on the Hohe Strasse?" Hunkeler asked.

"*Mais oui. Schön langsam*, slowly does it. I still have to get home too. Bye."

Hunkeler chugged along through the falling snow, gradually growing more content again. Having to listen to Pfister's xenophobic ranting had worn him out. His friend had been murdered and the idiot was getting worked up about four dead ducks.

The world was all bleak and deserted as he drove along the Hohe Strasse. Like in Siberia, he thought. No smoking chimneys, no warm hearth. Then the turn-off to his village appeared, with the St Imbert cross by the side of the path. He parked in front of his house and went in. Quickly and quietly, he got undressed and crept into Hedwig's bed, as soft-footed as a tomcat.

Hunkeler drove back to Basel early the next morning. He didn't go up to his apartment, just fetched his cross-country skis from the cellar. He briefly popped into the nearby Sommereck to read the newspapers. Edi was sitting at the regulars' table, sulking, with a glass of fruit juice in front of him. "Here, read this," he said and passed Hunkeler the Zurich tabloid. "What a shambles. It's worse than in the Balkans."

"Stop it, will you? I'm fed up of hearing that rubbish. Just fetch us some coffee instead."

The title page showed a photo of Chalet Enzian. An arrow pointed at the gable. Title: "Corpse found hanging from meathook here". Question: *Who will be beheaded next?*

The text was by Hauser. Was it the work of Islamists? Did they come from a terrorist training camp near Mulhouse? Is the Basel police slacking?

"It's dreadful what's happening in our Basel," moaned Edi. "Nobody's safe any more, not even within their own four walls."

"Stop it now. Eat something instead."

"I'm not allowed, remember? They've put me on a muesli diet. Just oat flakes with bran."

"Who gives a shit?" shouted Hunkeler. "You'll just have to eat bran then." He threw the tabloid into the corner and picked up the *Basler Zeitung*. Their report was very restrained. The crime had been committed in France rather than on Basel soil. Hence the Police Nationale was responsible. The Basel Criminal Investigation Department would of course be assisting with the case. Next to the text was a photo of Prosecutor Suter, in his yellow ski jumper. "I'm sorry," said Hunkeler. "I didn't mean to shout at you."

"But you did. I can't take it on an empty stomach. By the way, I happen to have a delicacy from Alsace in the house. A pheasant pâté from Illhäusern. You won't find anything like that in a shop."

"Bring it out then. Let's polish it off."

Edi fetched some fresh bread and the pheasant pâté.

He tucked in as if he hadn't seen food for days. The pâté really did taste fantastic. "Now it's gone," he said sorrowfully. "Back to being hungry."

At ten, Hunkeler turned off from the motorway towards the Emmental. It was snowing without pause. He crossed the bridge at Aarwangen and looked out over the gently steaming waters of the Aare. This was where they used to stop off on their summer trips, him, his wife and his daughter. They would wander upstream along the river and then drift back down again in the cool water. Those were good times, and yet he didn't long to have them back.

To the left stood the black stone tower of the old castle, where for centuries prisoners condemned by the rulers in Bern had languished until their deaths. He drove through Langenthal and into the agricultural lands, dotted with mighty farmsteads. At the Hirsernbad country inn, he parked and set about fitting the snow chains onto the wheels. He cursed loudly when the first chain fell off the wheel, like a lumberjack whose axe had hit a stone. The cursing made him grin. That would never stop, he simply was and always would be short-tempered, and that was fine by him.

When the chains were firmly in place, lashed tight by the rubber straps, he decided to knock back a drink. He went in, sat down at the table nearest the fire and ordered a glass of Beaujolais. As he sipped his wine, he contemplated the three Swiss confederates hewn into the sandstone above the hearth. Rendered in the style of naive peasant art, the confederates had just five legs between them.

He was glad to have escaped from the allotments. He took his phone out of his pocket and switched it off. Good, now he could no longer be reached.

Contentedly, he carried on driving up the valley. The farmsteads looked even more imposing in the white land-scape. As he drove past one of them, he opened the car window and inhaled the smell of silage. He tried to whoop in jubilation, but all that came out was a hoarse croak. Those damned cigarettes. He reached into his pocket and threw his packet out of the window.

Up by the Bären inn he turned off towards Lueg. He drove into fog so thick he couldn't see more than ten yards. Carefully he steered the car along the ruts that had formed in the snow. He cruised past farms where black dogs ran out to chase his car. He didn't stop at the Lueg viewpoint, there was nothing to see. On he rolled, until he reached the Kaltacker inn. There he got out, put on his cross-country skis and set off. Straight across the meadows, through the deep, fluffy snow. His pulse hammering, he stomped onwards like a Canadian trapper. At one point, a dog came running up to him, barking inquisitively. It seemed pleased to have found a companion. "Come on, Bäri!" Hunkeler called out. "Come with me, we'll race across the prairie to the natives!" The dog yowled and rolled over in the snow, then stayed behind.

Hunkeler reached the edge of a woodland and stopped. He realized he'd lost all sense of direction. He no longer knew which way was south and which was north. He'd never experienced this before. There was nothing but the tall trunks of the pine trees, with their dark crowns that let slide a lump of snow every now and then. No bird, not a single sound. He waited a while until his pulse had calmed down. Then he turned round and followed his tracks back to the Kaltacker.

It was a beautiful old inn, built from wood like everything else up here. There was no shortage of pines. He inhaled the familiar scent of resin. The picture of General Guisan was still hanging on the wall. In the eyes of the people here, he had won the Second World War. There was a Sumiswald clock and a picture of four men playing a game of jass, each slamming a card on the table. PLAY RAMSEN HERE was written on a slate board.

Today's lunch was Flädli soup, followed by calf's head in vinaigrette with boiled potatoes and endive salad. He ordered a half-bottle of mineral water and a glass of Mâcon Chardonnay from the barrel. He ate with care, wary at first, unsure whether the calf's head had been cooked thoroughly. It was tender but not overdone, there was still some bite to it. It was served with finely chopped onions in vinegar.

"Damn good," he said to the landlady when she brought him a second glass of Mâcon.

"Just a pity it's snowing so heavily," she replied. "Nobody's going to come up here in this murky weather."

He stayed sitting there for half an hour, in silence. He heard the clock strike on the wall and a cow mooing in the barn next door.

He drove back across the Lueg to Affoltern, took a room at the Sonne inn and lay down on the bed. He fell fast asleep and didn't wake up until three.

At half past three, Hunkeler entered the local council offices of Rüegsau, to which Rüegsbach belonged. An elderly woman greeted him and asked what he wanted. To enquire about a citizen of Rüegsbach by the name of Anton Flückiger, he replied. He showed her his badge.

"Aha, another copper," she commented. "I've already had one on the phone this morning, someone from Mulhouse in Alsace. Yes, well, Tönu. It was bound to end badly."

"Why?"

"Because he was always chasing after the womenfolk. The men won't tolerate that."

"But the women tolerated it?"

"Of course," she replied. "Don't ask me why, but they all liked him."

"So what kind of man was he?"

She pondered a while. There was no depth in her dark eyes, no shine. "He was a sweet man. Kind and affectionate. And very open. Up here, the men can be so buttoned-up."

"Didn't he have a proper sweetheart?" he asked. "Someone special to stay with?"

"He did, Sonja Flückiger. She had a grocery store up by the bend in the road. It's closed now, but she still lives there. He stayed with her for a few years. Until he had to leave. They sent him away. It was a tragedy. People say that Ursli, that's her son, was his, you see."

"I see. Is that why he took on the name Flückiger?"

"I think so. He needed a proper name. His original name supposedly was Livius. Some say he was Russian. But you'd best talk to Beat Jau. He's our mayor. He's here, just a moment." She walked towards the door in the background.

"There was one more thing I was going to ask, if I may," said Hunkeler.

"Yes?" She looked at him expectantly, as if hoping for help.

"*AK*," he said. "Küssu, Köbu, Wäutu, Fridu, Ülu, Tönu. Do those names mean anything to you?"

"Yes, of course. *AK*, the Alten Kameraden. Or the Alten Kanonen."

"I don't understand."

"He had some wacky ideas, Tönu Flückiger. He was a bit crazy. But never in a weird way, always funny. People up here are glad when there's something going on for once.

They join in. But they would never have come up with the idea themselves."

"Come up with what idea?"

"When he first came here, Tõnu lived at Hinterglatt. At the Niklausens' farm, with Wäutu and Fridu. Küssu, Köbu and Ülu lived there too. They had this old cannon there. It's supposed to be from Näppu's times."

"Näppu?"

"From the time of Napoleon. Tõnu fired it, up on the Glöris, always on certain special days. On 21 March, I think, on 21 June and on 21 September. They always had a great big party up on the Glöris, they'd light a fire, guzzle beer. He talked them into it, and they joined in. They were the Alten Kanonen." She paused to see if he was listening. Then she carried on. "You could hear the cannon thunder all over the area, always around midnight. Three times they'd fire it. And people thought, they're crazy, those men up at Hinterglatt."

"And you? What did you think?"

She considered whether she could say what she wanted to say. She hadn't shifted her gaze from him a single time. "It was fun. When does anything ever happen up here? Almost never, nothing ever happens. And when something does happen, it's something really bad."

"And in winter, did they do it in winter too?" he asked.

"No, not in winter. The nights around 21 December are the holy nights. That's when the men go to the inn to play Rams. And in the week after Christmas they go to the Kalter Markt, the fair in Sumiswald. That's nothing for us women."

Pity, thought Hunkeler. He wondered whether he should invite the woman to dinner. But that probably wouldn't go down too well with an outsider, especially a copper.

"And Ursli, how is he?"

She looked at him for a long time. A shadow passed before her gaze, even darker than her eyes. "I don't know. Nobody here knows. All we know is that he's not buried here in our cemetery."

"Then where is he?"

"Somewhere in Zurich, they say. Got in with the addicts in Platzspitz Park."

The door behind her opened and a large, elderly man appeared. He eyed Hunkeler suspiciously, then gave the woman a cross look. "What is it, Frau Lüscher?"

"This is a police officer from Basel," she replied. "He's come about Tönu Flückiger."

"And? What have you told him?"

"Just the basics."

"Aha? Well, you'd better come in then." He led the way into his office and sat down on the chair behind his desk. "Who are you?"

Hunkeler placed his badge on the desk.

"OK. What do you want?"

"You already know that," Hunkeler replied. "And it wouldn't harm you to be a bit more friendly."

"True, it wouldn't," said Jau. "But why should I? We've had nothing but trouble with him. And now we have more trouble."

"Not true. It's us that have the trouble, we from the Basel CID."

"But we end up in the newspapers. We don't want that. And anyway, we don't like Basel police officers up here."

"I'm not from Basel."

"Yes, I can hear that. Where from?"

"From Aargau. We used to rent a little chalet near here for twelve years, from Alfred Held. Just outside Affoltern."

"Ah, there." He got up and moved a chair in front of the desk. "There you go, sit down."

Hunkeler sat.

"A guy from Mulhouse rang this morning," Jau said. "I didn't tell him anything."

"Nothing stays secret up here," Hunkeler pointed out. "I can just go and talk to people."

"We used to have six dairies in this parish," said Jau. "Now we have one, and it's not clear whether that will survive either. Barely anyone can make a living in the dairy industry these days. People have to get a side job. We used to have proud, autonomous farms here. We ran them how we saw fit. Many a thing wasn't done the correct, official way, including the paperwork. Today every government office and every outside department wants to interfere."

"I understand where you're coming from," said Hunkeler. "But it's better you talk to me than to someone else."

Jau studied the fingernails on his left hand. They seemed to be clean. Then he studied the fingernails on his right hand. "True," he said. "So ask."

"What was Anton Flückiger's previous name? And why did you grant him citizenship?"

"Anton Livius turned up here in September 1952. All he had with him was a small, brown leather suitcase. The Niklausens at Hinterglatt took him in. He worked on the farm in return for board and lodging and some pocket money. Nobody asked about it. Fellows like him used to turn up regularly. They would stay for a few weeks and then move on. He told us he was from Tilsit. And that he'd been a soldier. That's all he said. He had an old German passport that confirmed this. My father, Konrad Jau, was mayor at the time. He told me this. Apparently the passport was barely legible, the photo no longer identifiable. As if it had been lying in the rain for months. There was no reason not to trust the man. He was a good worker, he pulled his weight."

"Do you think Livius was his real name?"

"How should I know? In any case, he lost his passport soon afterwards. This didn't bother us, we don't set much store by papers. Then he met a woman, Sonja Flückiger, from Rinderbach. He moved in with her and worked for Dres, in the joiner's workshop. Dres said he was happy with him. Sonja gave birth to a son, Urs. The boy was his. Up to that point, everything was OK."

"Why didn't they get married?"

"Because it wasn't possible. He didn't have any papers. But my father liked things to be neat and tidy, so he suggested Anton should be granted citizenship. Under the name of his future wife. And so that's what the district council decided to do."

"He could have kept his real name."

"We were happy with it. Livius from Rüegsbach, that would have sounded very odd. Also, he said he wanted to leave his old life behind and start a new one. And for this he needed a new name."

"So you granted him citizenship, just like that? I thought the Emmental people are quite conservative."

"We don't care. We take people as we find them. And we found him to be OK. He had good friends in the area. People liked him."

"Ah yes. The Alten Kanonen."

This made Jau grin, the memory of the cannon blasts seemed to amuse him. "He was always up to something. But then he started taking things too far. People here don't like that."

"Taking things too far in what way?"

Jau studied his fingernails some more. "That's nobody's business."

"They say he was Russian originally."

"I don't know anything about that." Jau had said all he was willing to say. End of story.

"Did he leave of his own accord?"

"When we want someone gone from the parish, we have ways to make that happen."

"And Urs? What happened to him?"

"Urs disappeared. Anything else? I need to get back to work now. Thank you."

Hunkeler drove back towards Affoltern, nice and steady, so he wouldn't miss the turn-off. It was getting dark. The lights of the Restaurant Krone glided by and the last few houses passed from sight. Just darkness all around, and snowflakes dancing in the glare of the headlights.

Then he saw the signpost to Hinterglatt on the right. He turned off and changed down into first gear. He followed the tyre tracks, which were faintly visible. It was probably crazy, driving up here to visit complete strangers. He could easily get stuck in the snow. He didn't care. A couple of times, he felt the wheels sliding, then the snow chains would grip again.

He came into some woods where the snow wasn't as deep. To the left and right, icicles flashed in the beam of his headlights. He passed a pebbly rock face, strangely shapeshifting due to the large chunks of protruding gravel and the roots of a fir tree that clung to it. He crossed a ten-yard stretch of ice, probably from a brook that had frozen over. Then he found himself on an open field where the snow lay virtually untouched. He ploughed through it like a barge.

He felt the buildings drawing near before he saw them. Perhaps he could smell them, or he'd heard a sound, a bark or mooing. He rolled onto a courtyard with a towering lime tree. He recognized it as such by its hefty trunk and its bark, the branches above were hidden in the dark. He stopped and got out.

There were three farmhouses and various outbuildings. The lights were on in the kitchens. A St Bernard came limping towards him, an old animal. It gave a hoarse bark and bared its teeth. Then it let Hunkeler ruffle its fur, yipping with pleasure.

Hunkeler waited several minutes. Finally, one of the kitchen doors opened. A girl with dyed yellow plaits came out. She looked across at the stranger. "Come, Teddu," she said. "Leave him be."

The dog went over to her and licked her hand.

"What is it?" she asked. "Are you looking for someone?"

"I'm looking for Wäutu or Fridu," said Hunkeler.

"Fridu is in the cowshed, back there."

She pointed round to the right of the house and disappeared back into the kitchen with the dog.

Hunkeler walked round the side of the house. He caught a glimpse into the living room, where he saw an old woman sitting in an armchair; he passed two privies positioned above the slurry pit and a pigsty with grunting pigs. He heard the hum of milking machines, the rattling of chains, then he entered the cowshed.

Two dozen dairy cows stood lined up, Simmentals with pale brown markings. They had poked their heads through the bars and were eating. There was no gutter, the cow dung fell through a grate onto a belt that led to the dungheap. Two light bulbs, two milking machines, two men with milking stools on their backsides. One old, one young, obviously father and son. They looked at him.

"Who's Fridu?" Hunkeler asked. "I'm looking for Fridu."

"Me," said the old one. "What the devil's going on? What's wrong?"

"Nothing's going on, I just want to talk to you," Hunkeler replied. "My name is Peter and I'm a Basel police officer."

"Take a seat then."

Hunkeler sat down on the bench by the wall and waited. The two men quietly carried on working, positioning the teat cups, crouching down beside a cow to prepare her.

"How's life in Basel?" Fridu asked after a while. "By the way, this is Küssu, my son."

"Not too bad, thanks," Hunkeler replied. "Handsome goods you have there."

"Yes, the goods are handsome all right. But nobody wants them any more. I'm in my seventies, I don't care. But Küssu, he cares."

"Yes," Küssu agreed.

"Küssu, Köbu, Wäutu, Fridu, Ülu, Tönu," said Hunkeler. "We found a postcard with those names on it. It has a picture of the fair in Sumiswald in 1958."

"That was a different Küssu," Fridu told him. "That was his uncle. He's dead. The others are dead too, I'm the only one still alive. And now Tönu is dead too. I'm the last Alte Kanone." He laughed, almost silently, but he was in stitches. Küssu joined in, also barely making a sound. Then they calmed down again.

"That's life," said Fridu. "Why did they tear his head off?"

"That's exactly what I want to find out," Hunkeler replied. "And you need to help me."

"How?"

"What was Anton Flückiger's real name?"

"Livius, as far as I know."

"I don't believe that," said Hunkeler.

"Why not?"

"I think he kept his real name secret. Because he was frightened."

"Of what?"

"I don't know."

Fridu removed the teat cups from an udder, checked to see if they were OK, shuffled to the next cow and reattached them.

"This is high-tech, this milking machine," he said. "It stops all by itself when the udder is empty." And then, after a while: "Well, it's possible."

Hunkeler waited. He could feel himself growing sleepy, here in this barn. The warmth of the animals' bodies, their slow chomping, the dung falling to the ground, the calm, measured movements of the men as they worked. But he stayed wide awake.

"He was a strange old bird, Tönu. A proper oddball. Yes, I think he probably was afraid of something. He never talked about it. But something from his past troubled him. Something he couldn't come to terms with. He was a little too jolly, he went a bit over the top with the jolliness. We liked it. None of us would have ever come up with the idea of firing the cannon. Why would we? You could hear the blasts far across the valley. Not everyone liked that. We didn't care. When he was gone, we stopped doing it. At some point we heard he was working in a warehouse in Basel. We never saw him again."

"Why did he go away?"

"He didn't go away. He was sent away."

"Why?"

"I reckon you've probably been to see Beat Jau. And he didn't tell you anything."

"You're right."

"Why should I tell you anything?"

"Because you know."

"Did you drive up here especially for that?" Fridu asked.

"Yes."

"Nobody else drives up here," said Fridu. "Not even the tanker truck that collects the milk. Not in this snow. Tönu was a wild fella. He was troubled somehow. He had a good woman, Sonja. It all went well in the beginning. But then he started making moves on other women. The wife of the old parish clerk, for example. I know that for sure. And there were rumours he had something going on with old Jau's wife. The gentlemen don't look too kindly on that. They dunked him."

"What's that?"

"They sent out the lads, who chucked him in the stream. Again and again. Until he left. I liked Tönu. I still miss him even now. Does this information help you?"

"A little, yes," said Hunkeler.

Fridu turned off the milking machine. Only the chomping of the cows could still be heard. "Fetch the Jeep," he said. "Time to load up." Küssu went out. Fridu undid the belt of his milking stool and hung it on a hook above the bench. "Seventy years of dairy farming," he said. "Seventy years of mowing, haymaking, milking, driving the milk to the dairy. Every morning, every evening. And what do you get for it?" He spat on the floor. "Do you know how to play Rams?" he asked.

"I used to," replied Hunkeler. "But in Aargau we only played it on 21 December. We kept going until four in the morning, though."

"It's different round here. We play it in the week after Christmas. But you can also play Rams in the week after New Year, until Epiphany. Come to the Säge in Rinderbach this evening, we'll have a round."

"I will."

Outside, the Jeep could be heard pulling up.

"Go and see Sonja up on the bend," said Fridu. "She knows his name."

Hunkeler drove back to the main road. There was no one else about. He didn't pass any tractors, no horse and cart that might be taking the full milk pails to the dairy. That was all done by the tanker truck now. Except at Fridu's place, when there were three feet of snow on the ground. Cheese production had been streamlined through and through, and still it didn't pay. He resolved to eat more Emmentaler.

He passed the Säge inn and the joinery workshop beside it. This was where Livius had worked, and in such a manner that Dres had been happy with him. He could have had a quiet life with Sonja. What had got in the way? Was he really from Russia? And what would that have signified in the imagination of the people up here? That he was an energetic, wild man, a Cossack, a Tatar, a wild fella, as Fridu had said. But where did his fear stem from, his urge to flee, to hide, to change his own name?

As the road started to climb and loop round, he saw to his left a small wooden house with a shop front. This must be the shop on the bend. He turned off sharply and came to a stop in front of the window. He got out and looked around for signs of who might live here. There was nothing, no bell, no name. He rapped his fist on the door, three times. Then he waited. A little further down there was a street lamp. Its glow faintly penetrated the driving snow that was falling even more thickly now.

Eventually he saw a light in the hallway, coming closer. A key was turned in the lock, twice. The door opened, very slowly. An old woman stood before him, dimly illuminated by the paraffin lamp she held in her hand. Long, white hair, her eyes barely discernible. Sunken lips, front teeth missing. She was wearing a black coat and felt slippers on her feet. The woman raised the lamp. "Yes?"

"Good evening," Hunkeler replied. "May I come in?"

The woman directed the light at his face as best she could. She looked at him for a long time, immobile, her eyes lifeless. "Is it you?" she asked. "Are you coming home?"

"No," said Hunkeler. "I'm a stranger. But I'd like to come in."

She waited a while. She was probably hoping to remember and recognize him. Then she turned and shuffled back along the hallway.

He pulled the door closed behind him and followed her into the kitchen. There was a bricked-in wood stove with a fire burning in it. A coffee pot stood on the hotplate. Sink, cupboard, a table with two chairs. On it a vase with three paper flowers. Stacks of firewood lined the walls, branches for kindling, fir and beech logs.

"They cut my electricity," she said, "because I didn't pay the bills. I have to buy the paraffin myself. The wood I get from Fridu, at least there's that. Sit down."

Hunkeler sat and watched as the old woman removed the pot from the stove and set it on the table. She took two cups from the sink, rubbed them clean and poured the coffee. A tin of sugar stood on the table.

"What brings you here?" she asked.

He took a spoonful of sugar from the tin and stirred it into the cup. He drank slowly. It was a concoction made from a lot of chicory and very little coffee. "I've come from Basel," he said. "I'm a police officer. I've come about Tönu."

She had watched him closely, her gaze following him as he moved. Now she took her time as she, in turn, stirred sugar into her cup. "They stole him from me," she said. "I complained, but they didn't give him back."

"You know that he's dead?"

She gently shook her head, then she giggled briefly. She lifted her cup with both hands, took two gulps and set down the cup again. "I live off this brew," she said. "It's all I have, apart from potatoes. Dead, what does that mean anyway? He disappeared a long time ago. Just like Ursli.

One went to Basel, the other to Zurich. Neither of them visits me. Neither of them is buried here. The cemetery is full of strangers. Why don't you arrest them?"

"Who should I arrest?"

"Jau. And the old parish clerk too. They sent him away. Why don't they take better care of their women? Wimps, that's what they are. They have no idea about women. Every cow in their barn is dearer to them, every goat. All they can do with a woman is insult her. Because they're afraid of her. Tönu was different. He was a proper Russian, he had a big heart. That was what frightened them."

"Are the three roses from him?"

She nodded. "He won them for me. At a shooting stall at the fair in Sumiswald. Always with the first shot. He was good at it, he'd learned to shoot because he had to protect himself. He always had a gun with him, one from the war. Only I knew that. If he'd wanted to, he could have easily defended himself against the young louts who threw him into the stream. But he said he didn't want to shoot anyone any more, not unless there was no other way. He preferred to disappear." Again, she giggled. There was a hint of pride there, the pride of an old, faithful girl. "He screamed in the middle of the night. Then he'd wake up with a start and cling to me so tightly I could hardly breathe. That's how much he loved me."

"What was he afraid of? Surely he was safe here in the Emmental."

She shook her head, slowly. A delicate blush crept across her face. He could see she was making an effort to lie. "He wouldn't tell me. Not for anything in the world. Perhaps I could have helped him, who knows?"

A silent stillness enveloped the room. Not even the ticking of a clock could be heard.

Suddenly, there was a rustling sound. It came from the wall behind the cupboard. A mouse appeared on the batten that ran along the wall. It knew the way. It progressed quickly, jumped onto the table, then made a beeline for the tin. That was its final destination. The mouse tried several times, but kept falling back down onto the table. It was just too funny, Hunkeler burst out laughing.

The old woman seemed to have been expecting the mouse. She had watched the animal closely as it tried to climb up and kept sliding down. Now she was startled. It must have been a long time since she'd heard anyone laugh. She tried to join in with a smile, but it didn't quite work. "That's my pet," she said. "We get along very well." She took her spoon and sprinkled some sugar onto the table. The mouse tucked in, it seemed to be enjoying it. "Perhaps he would still be here with me, if he could have told me," she said. She stood up, opened the lower door of the cupboard and took out a dusty box of biscuits. She fetched a pair of scissors from the drawer, cut open the packet and placed it on the table. "Here, this is all I can offer you."

He took a biscuit. It crumbled in his hand, it was probably decades old. He wolfed it down. "But you know his name, don't you?" he said.

The blush vanished from her face, it turned lily-white again. In the light of the paraffin lamp, only her eyes glimmered, curiously triumphant, full of hidden wiles. "He was called Livius. Then he took my name, Anton Flückiger." She placed a biscuit next to the mouse. It sniffed at it and tried to carry it off, but only half succeeded. The mouse couldn't get onto the batten with it.

"I mean before," he said. "When he still lived in Tilsit."

She looked at him openly now. She had a secret. And this secret kept her alive. "Why should I tell you his name?"

"Because his gravestone should bear his real name."

"In fidelity, faith and defiance," she said. "All his life they tried to break him. All his life he fought back. They took everything from him. He had no money, no occupation, no passport. He worked hard, he made himself useful. But when all was said and done, he was an outlaw. All he had was me. And his real name. That's the only thing they didn't get from him."

The mouse had given up trying to haul away the biscuit and set about eating it there and then.

"Fidelity, faith and defiance," said Hunkeler. "Where did you get those words from?"

"They are the three truths of the rose."

Shortly before eight, Hunkeler parked in front of the Säge and went inside. Three tables were occupied by card players engrossed in their games of Rams. They were competing for smoked sausages and sides of bacon, which were laid out on a side table.

He ordered a bratwurst with onions and a bottle of beer. He thought of Sonja Flückiger, the ancient girl with the long, white hair who lived off chicory coffee and potatoes. But still she hadn't betrayed her dead lover.

117

When he'd finished eating, Fridu came in with two others. They joined Hunkeler at his table and played doggedly, without talking. They fought for every trick. Twelve sausages were claimed. One of them was won by Hunkeler. It wasn't much, but still. He wouldn't have liked to leave the battleground with no trophy at all. Several times he'd forgotten the particular rules of this game. That the *Belli*, the seven of diamonds, was always the second highest trump. That you had to follow suit, and trump if you couldn't. He was too tired to persevere against the measured ferocity of his fellow players. Or his mind wasn't on the job.

He drank another bottle of beer. At one point, when he had to excuse himself, Fridu came with him. "Did she tell you?"

"No," said Hunkeler.

"Dammit," Fridu replied. "Why not?"

"Because she's too proud."

"And now you're going to drive back to Basel?"

"What else can I do?"

"That stubborn cow," said Fridu. "That's typical of Sonja. She could have easily got married when he was gone. Even though she had Ursli. But she refused point-blank." He fiddled around adjusting his clothes. Then he took a carpenter's pencil from his pocket and wrote something on the mirror. It was a name. Russius. He took his handkerchief and wiped the name off again. "I didn't tell you anything."

When Hunkeler woke the next morning, the sun was shining in his face. He struggled to get his bearings at first. Then he saw the sausage hanging on the bedpost. He grinned contentedly. He'd managed to snatch one at least. And now he was lying in a hotel bed in Affoltern.

He stayed tucked up under the red and white checked eiderdown for a little longer. He thought of Sonja and how she had given the village heavyweights the finger.

Then, looking at the sausage again, he thought how he would leave it to simmer, an hour and a half over a low heat, with dried beans, summer herbs, onions and garlic. Hedwig would be pleased.

He got up and walked across the creaking floorboards to the window. He tore it wide open and inhaled the icy-cold air. A snow-covered field stretched out in front of him, gleaming in the morning sun, fringed by the wintry forest. Towering beyond were the Bernese Alps with the Eiger, the Mönch and the Jungfrau. The north face of the Eiger in dark shade, the drawn-out peak of the Jungfrau in blazing light. He felt moved to whoop again, but that probably wouldn't work straight after waking up.

He breakfasted downstairs in the public room. Bacon and two fried eggs, the yolks still runny, slightly domed, served with freshly baked bread and a pot of black tea. He sprinkled salt and a little pepper over the eggs and chomped away contentedly.

Three farmers sat at the next table. They were talking about Tönu Flückiger, they had read something in the tabloid lying on the table. Hunkeler only listened with half an ear, he didn't want to think about it yet. But then he went and fetched the paper anyway.

"Was a doppelgänger beheaded?" the headline read. "Who was the real Anton Livius? What is Rüegsbach hiding?"

The questions, and the article beneath them, were by Hauser. There was a picture of Rüegsbach, showing the village in summer. So Hauser hadn't been up here yet. But he'd beaten Basel CID to it again. How the devil had he managed that, Hunkeler wondered. I'm going to punch the guy's lights out, he thought. He dabbed some bread at the last remnants of egg yolk, rinsed it down with a gulp of tea and reached into his pocket for a cigarette. Finding none, he gave up on the idea.

He read Hauser's article. Hauser had found out that Anton Flückiger couldn't possibly be the same person as Anton Livius. The real Livius was also born in 1922 and also came from Tilsit, but he had been a tank driver and was killed in action near Kharkiv in 1943. The implications were obvious. Anton Flückiger had obtained Livius' passport by whatever crooked means and had claimed it as his own. He had adopted another man's identity. Why? Because he wanted to hide. And why did he want to hide? Because he feared punishment or revenge.

That meant the Rüegsbach authorities hadn't given shelter to an upstanding and honourable man, as district mayor Beat Jau had claimed over the phone, but to a dark element, a crook, perhaps even a war criminal. These, concluded Hauser, were the consequences of rashly granted citizenship. Well meant, but leading to a bad end. And: we will keep digging.

It was probably time to get out of here, thought Hunkeler. Soon Hauser would turn up with his crafty colleagues. They would visit Fridu at his farm and sit down with Sonja in her kitchen. A hot story like this, about a shady foreigner who had infiltrated the Emmental idyll, was far too good to miss out on.

The three men at the next table had stopped talking when he'd fetched the newspaper. "What's up?" one of them said. "Aren't you the Basel police officer who played Rams in the Säge yesterday?"

"Yes," replied Hunkeler. "Why?"

"We don't like Basel pigs."

When he wanted to pay, the landlord came to Hunkeler's table. "No need," he said. "You'd better go now."

Hunkeler laid a hundred-franc note on the table and stood up. The landlord took the note and held it up against the sunlight falling through the window.

"That's counterfeit," he said. "We have no use for this up here." He tore the banknote into four pieces and laid them in the ashtray.

Hunkeler went out and got into his car. He felt a bit shaky, even though he knew the men wouldn't have thumped him. A police officer was still the long arm of the law, even if they called him a pig. No police officer had been assaulted here since the peasants' war.

As he drove down to Häusernmoos, a smile spread across his face. Unbelievable, he thought, the many different worlds that made up Switzerland. He knew the crafty boys from Zurich would have a tough time of it up here. They might be cheeky and clever, but so were the people of Rüegsbach.

The road had recently been treated and he made good progress. He overtook a horse-drawn sleigh along the way. It had come from a restaurant in Weiher where you could eat roast ham and ploughman's fillet, according to the sign on the rear of the sleigh. As if a ploughman had ever eaten fillet.

At the Hirsernbad he stopped for an espresso. He looked

over at the three Swiss confederates with their five legs. It's OK, he thought, you carry on sticking together. We'll still get to the truth.

He leafed through the Bern newspaper. There was nothing in there about Livius. The next two or three days would show whether the tabloid was going to succeed in making the Livius case a story of national interest. For that they would need fresh material, something new every day.

He took the phone out of his pocket, switched it on and rang Lüdi.

"Yes?"

"It's me, Hunkeler. I'm at the Hirsernbad, having coffee. Any news?"

He heard the chuckle, which never boded well. "You're good," said Lüdi. "There you are, feasting on bratwurst and rösti and having a cosy time being snowed in. Meanwhile all hell breaks loose here."

"What kind of hell?"

"Didn't you read the tabloid?"

"Yes, I did. They chucked me out, up in Affoltern. But it was obvious Flückiger wasn't Livius."

"Well, try telling Bardet that. Suter was in a rage too. And rightly so, I would say. Why is that damned Hauser always faster than us? Do you know?"

"Because he has connections," replied Hunkeler, "and money. One hand washes the other, and each hand is dirty. Who did you enquire with?"

"The military history research office in Potsdam and the military archive in Freiburg im Breisgau. They were closed over the holidays. We didn't get a reply from them until this morning. Everything Hauser wrote is true."

"Well, that's OK then," said Hunkeler. "What else?"

"Nothing is OK, absolutely nothing. We have no control over anything. Last night, Ferati's cabin was set on fire."

Another short chuckle, barely audible.

"Will you stop that stupid chuckling," Hunkeler shouted so loudly the landlady looked across at him.

"I can't, you know that," said Lüdi. "Imagine what Hauser is going to write tomorrow. The fiery fingers of terror. The hand of revenge reaches up from the grave. We're providing him with all the headlines he could possibly want."

"Not us," said Hunkeler. "The past is doing that. It's resurfacing."

"Quit philosophizing, will you? Madörin has locked up Beat Pfister. And Dogan too. They're both due to be arraigned. Madörin is insisting on it."

"He's such an idiot," Hunkeler barked, then nodded at the landlady. "Sorry."

"You don't need to apologize," said Lüdi. "Just get back here. The briefing is at four."

Hunkeler was silent. He was weighing up how much he should say. "His name is Russius," he told Lüdi. "Anton Russius."

Silence on the line. No chuckle, nothing.

"Are you still there?"

"Yes," Lüdi replied. "Are you sure? Who gave you that?"

"I can't tell you. And something else. We need to keep it under wraps. Otherwise Hauser will turn all of Rüegsbach on its head. They don't deserve that."

"But I have to work with it."

"Yes, of course. It would be best if you could find out as much as possible by four today."

"OK, I'll try. Who should I tell?"

"Nobody. Not until four."

"What about Bardet?"

"To hell with Bardet."

It turned into one of the most tense briefings Hunkeler had ever experienced. No police officer, whether French or Swiss, liked to be upstaged by a journalist. They'd all suffered a blow to their ego. They sat there full of resentment, ready to lash out at the first opportunity, without knowing who or what to lash out at.

It was this barely controlled, helpless aggression that made Hunkeler long for retirement. He wanted no more to do with it. Enough now, stop. He was glad he didn't have to report. Lüdi was going to take care of that.

Prosecutor Suter opened the meeting. He did it with confidence, demonstrating his brilliance once more. The situation was very serious, he said. Not just because of the unsolved murder case, but primarily because of the competition from the press. There was a risk that both crime departments, Mulhouse and Basel, would be made a laughing stock. The state's monopoly on the legitimate use of force went hand in hand with an investigative monopoly. This monopoly had to be maintained under all circumstances. It was time, he added, to stop with the turf war.

Madame Godet concurred.

Commissaire Bardet spoke next. He was in a foul mood and kept it very brief.

Point one, the autopsy had largely been completed. It was confirmed that Flückiger had been shot at close range. The murder weapon was most likely to be an officer's handgun from the time after the Second World War. This had not yet been verified, however. The murder was committed between 2 and 3 a.m. The victim had an old tattoo of a rose under his left upper arm. His blood alcohol level was 0.18 per cent. Traces of Viagra had also been detected, but no evidence of coitus. A box of Viagra pills had been found in Flückiger's apartment.

"What are you playing at?" Madörin interjected, red-faced with anger. "Why are you feeding us trivia?"

Bardet continued undeterred.

Point two, a range of different shoe prints had been secured. These might lead to information on who hung Flückiger up. It was conceivable that a single man could have done this, alone. In particular, they had found prints from sports shoes, the kind popular with young men. One possibility was that these young men had entered the allotments from the north, so from Alsace.

Point three, they had also secured a number of fingerprints. Drinking bouts had evidently taken place on New Year's Eve, not just on B35 but in other cabins too. People had gone round visiting each other, which was a New Year's Eve tradition in the allotments. So far, they had established that Füglistaller, Stebler, Siegrist, Pfister, Dogan and Cattaneo had visited B35.

Point four, they had now managed to speak to the people of B26 by phone. They were flying back to Basel on Sunday,

8 January. Unfortunately there were no grounds to demand an earlier return.

Point five, the French consul in Thailand had confirmed that several German pensioners residing at the Sunshine Inn in Phuket had been washed into the sea by the Boxing Day tsunami. These were the verified particulars they had so far, thanks in part to the kind support of Basel CID.

"Why aren't we allowed into the allotments?" Madörin asked.

"Good question," said Bardet. "Yes indeed, why not? We also found shoe prints that could well stem from an over-zealous investigator who arrived at the scene before us. From a Basel police detective, for example."

"That's enough," Suter said sharply. "What are you trying to suggest?"

"*Je vous en prie, Messieurs*," said Madame Godet. "*Restez tranquilles*. We're already *dans la merde*. How do you say that?"

"In the shit," volunteered contact man Morath.

Nobody said anything more for a while. They all knew it was true.

"Right," said Lüdi. "I will briefly report on what we did this morning. As you know, Ferati's cabin burned down last night. Unfortunately, our team hasn't been given access to the site. It seems certain that it was arson."

"Correct," Bardet confirmed. "They used gasoline."

Madörin blew his top. "And where did this gasoline come from?" he shouted. "Are there any tracks? And if so, where do these tracks lead to?"

"We are dealing with a murder case," said Madame Godet. "Not with the torching of a cabin."

"And what if the fire and the murder are linked, what then?" Madörin persisted.

"It's unbearable, all this screaming," commented Bardet and lit another cigarette. "Can't one do something about it?"

"I'm going to thrash you, Monsieur Bardet," yelled Madörin and smacked his fist on the table. "You'll be hearing from me. In the Zurich tabloids." He threw over his chair and walked out of the room.

"Sorry," said Suter. "He's lost all control. I will of course prevent him from doing any such thing."

"*Il est trop con,*" replied Bardet. "He's far too stupid."

"Perhaps if I could continue now," said Lüdi after he had picked up Madörin's chair. "Detective Sergeant Madörin arrested two of the allotment holders today. They are Messieurs Pfister and Godan."

"Why?" asked Madame Godet.

"Beat Pfister is a suspect because his ducks were killed. In Dogan's case, I don't have any specific information."

"Perhaps because he's a Kurd?" suggested Bardet. "It wouldn't look too good if just a Swiss was in custody, would it now?"

"What are you playing at?" Suter snarled.

"Quiet," Lüdi commanded. "All allotment holders have now been banned from entering the area. There are no more pet animals on the allotments that would require feeding. As I'm sure you can imagine, this restriction didn't go down well with some. Right. Let's talk about this Anton Livius."

"That's a real pickle you've got us into there," remarked Bardet.

"What pickle?" asked Suter.

"First you get hoodwinked by a con man with a fake passport."

Suter smiled sweetly. "That wasn't us," he said. "That was the Emmental authorities, fifty years ago."

"Was the passport fake or not? Well then. And now you've allowed a cheap tabloid journalist to outpace Basel CID by investigating faster and smarter."

"He was also faster than you."

"Because the holidays got in the way."

Now Suter lost his cool. "They got in our way too," he shouted.

"What? You mean you made your own enquiries?"

"Well, of course. Anton Flückiger was a Swiss citizen. Potsdam only got back to us at noon today, to say that he was not the same person as Livius."

"We got the same information," bellowed Bardet. "Also not until noon, but by then it was already in the newspaper."

"Quiet please," said Lüdi.

Suter and Bardet tried to compose themselves. Neither of them was used to being shouted at. If anyone did any shouting, it was them.

"I have something to say regarding Anton Flückiger," Lüdi continued. "The tabloid is right, his real name wasn't Livius. His real name was Anton Russius. Only we know that. Please treat this information as highly sensitive."

All colour drained from Bardet's face, he went deathly pale. "Where do you have this information from?"

"I drove to Rüegsbach yesterday," Hunkeler replied. "I asked the people there."

"I did too. I spoke to district mayor Jau on the phone. He didn't mention any such name."

"Sometimes it's best to turn up in person and talk to people face to face," Hunkeler commented.

"Can you name your specific source?" Bardet asked.

"I could, but I don't want to."

"Are you suggesting I can't be trusted?" Bardet barked.

"Hunkeler told me this morning on the phone," Lüdi went on. "I immediately got in touch with Potsdam. It didn't take long for them to find an Anton Russius from Tilsit who was sent to Holland and Czechoslovakia as an infantryman and who recuperated from a gunshot wound in Carlsbad. It seems he left the Wehrmacht on 12 August 1942. Then his trail goes cold."

"How was that possible?" asked Bardet. "Nobody got away from the Wehrmacht just like that."

"They're currently looking into that," Lüdi replied. "They said they'd call back tomorrow or the day after."

Everyone was silent. At least it was something, at least they had a firm lead.

"This probably puts all our previous findings in question," said Suter. "Also, please accept my sincere apologies for shouting earlier."

"I apologize in return," replied Bardet. "Once again, we face the fundamental question of whether the murder is directly linked to the allotment community or not."

"I suggest we let Madörin continue his work, but only in relation to the killing of Pfister's ducks and the torching of Ferati's cabin," said Suter. "I'll tell him to keep well away from B35."

"I couldn't agree more," Bardet replied. "We urgently need more facts about this Anton Russius. What did he do in August 1942? Where did he go? Did he hide out somewhere, and why? And above all, we need to prevent the hacks in Zurich from discovering his real name."

"How do you intend to prevent that?" asked Madame Godet.

"By going full steam ahead. We have to be so fast we can't be caught up with."

After the briefing, Hunkeler took Bardet by the arm. "Come. We need to talk."

They walked through the Steinenvorstadt quarter, where municipal workers were shovelling snow onto trucks. It had to be at least minus ten degrees. Bardet had wrapped his red scarf across the lower half of his face.

"Like Stalingrad," commented Hunkeler.

"*Merde*," muttered Bardet.

The trams on Barfüsserplatz were queuing up one behind the other all the way to the next stop. There was probably a frozen set of points up there.

They went into the Restaurant Kunsthalle and sat down at an elegantly laid table. A curious scent hung in the air, it smelled of greenhouse, of flowers. It came from the giant bouquet that stood in the centre of the room. The ice rink which the landlord had set up under the trees outside was buried under masses of snow. The plastic roof of the champagne bar had collapsed.

They ordered *entrecôte double* and a bottle of Chateau Rotie from the lower Rhône region. They talked very little, just brief exchanges about the wine and the meat. The quality was excellent, this they were agreed on.

"I'm sorry," said Hunkeler after a while. "I am who I am. And I don't intend to change at this stage. I'm a lone wolf and always will be."

"When did you find out?"

"Yesterday evening at midnight. In the toilets of an Emmental inn."

"Sixteen hours have passed since then. I mean between then and the briefing. Do you consider that acceptable? *C'est dégueulasse.* Absolutely disgusting."

"I switched off my phone when I headed out into the country," Hunkeler explained. "I tried to adjust to the rural rhythms. They live like in medieval times up there."

"They do have phones and email."

"True. But someone different wouldn't have got the name. I only succeeded because I completely cut myself off from Basel CID. I talked to a farmer in the back of beyond and won his trust. I sat in the kitchen of an ancient woman, Sonja Flückiger. It was her who took Russius in and gave him her name. They had a son together, he's passed away since. Russius won three roses for her at a shooting stall. They're still standing in a vase on her kitchen table. She lives with a mouse. The journalists from Zurich will find all of this out. But they won't get the name."

"You should have rung me this morning, at the very latest."

"I would have liked to keep the name to myself altogether," Hunkeler told him.

Bardet threw him a sharp look, full of suspicion. "You're a strange fellow."

"That's what my father used to tell me too," said Hunkeler.

"And what did you say in return?"

"I said I'm his son."

Bardet grinned at this, but only a little. "Still," he said. "That was improper. If I told the press you were keeping important information from me, there would be a great scandal."

"We have a name. I achieved that. And we have to keep this name under wraps. If you had rung Potsdam too, they would have got suspicious there. I think the tabloid has a direct line to Potsdam. May I?" He helped himself to one of Bardet's Caporal cigarettes. He felt dizzy at the first puff. "I lifted a secret. After lifting it, I kept it to myself for a little while. Because that's what I felt like doing."

"But you told Lüdi this morning."

"Not until I'd had a coffee at the Hirsernbad."

Bardet shook his head gruffly. "Tell me, what kind of person was your father? Can you describe him?"

Now it was Hunkeler's turn to grin, he felt a bit embarrassed. "There's a theory I've developed," he said. "A theory of mistakes. It's the only theory I believe in. I believe you can only achieve change through mistakes. Those who don't make mistakes don't change anything. Only mistakes are productive. Being faultless is fatal. So it's with a clear conscience that I beg your forgiveness."

"So be it then," replied Bardet. "Cheers."

At around 9 p.m., Hunkeler drove towards the border. It was Wednesday, 4 January. Hedwig was probably already in Colmar with Annette. He could have called her and asked what hotel she was staying in, which restaurant she was sitting in and what she'd had for dinner. He could have asked her how she was doing. How she was feeling after visiting the Unterlinden Museum, where Grünewald's Christ hung on the Cross, painted with such intimate precision in the colours of decay, long and appalling. Did she love him, he would have wanted to ask her, in the morning, in the evening and at night, even though he was an impossible bloke.

He let it be. He knew what she would have answered. She would have laughed in her warm voice, a voice he had fallen for straight away. Then she would have said: *It's your own fault you're not here.*

He was dog-tired. He'd had enough of driving through snowy nights, of staring at the glare of headlights on icy roads. He longed to lie down in his bed in Alsace. He would switch off his phone, open the window onto the garden as wide as it would go and listen to the owls calling to each other in the dark.

By the entrance to the allotments he saw Haller standing next to an Alsatian colleague. Hunkeler stopped. The Blume was dark and there were no lights on in the command vehicle either. A compressor could be heard from inside the allotments. "Any news?" he asked.

"No, other than that it's damned cold," Haller replied. "They're still digging on B35. God knows what they're looking for." He pointed across to where a gleam of light hovered over the allotments.

"And anything else afoot, apart from that?"

"Who would want to be afoot on a freezing night like this? Anyway, nobody's allowed to enter the allotments."

Hunkeler let the car roll on at a crawl. His headlights picked up the gravel silo, bulldozers, rusty trucks. Further ahead he could see a lamp glowing in the French custom house. He opened his window. A tiny light appeared behind the fence. Just for a second, then it was gone again. He waited a while to see whether the light would reappear. Nothing moved, the darkness remained undisturbed.

He parked up on the left, next to three wrecked cars. He took his gun out of the holster and placed it in the glove compartment. Then he got out and carefully closed the door. He looked up at the sky, at the myriad of twinkling stars. There was no moon, but the night was still bright.

He crossed the road to the fence and walked along it towards the custom house. After a few yards he saw the gap. Someone had cut the mesh and barbed wire and trimmed the hedge so there was enough space to crawl through. Again, the tiny light flashed.

He crawled through the gap. In front of him he saw the shadows of tracks in the snow. He got out his small flashlight and switched it on, shielding the beam with his hand. The footprints were from a man and a woman. There were other prints too, left by shoes with a rubber sole. They led in both directions, going in and out.

He considered whether to walk on or not. It was a good thing he'd left the gun in the car, he was here as a civilian.

He heard snow crunching underfoot and followed the sound. The crunching hadn't been caused by the rubber-soled shoes. They led off to the right, towards B35. He followed the footprints that led to the left, tracking a man and a woman. It was difficult to walk quietly. His feet kept breaking through the frozen layer under the fresh snow. He'd switched off his light, he could see the tracks without it. They led westwards, where Ferati's cabin had stood. He could smell the burned wood even from here. There was no sound now apart from the compressor, no light flashed.

He saw the gravel mound looming up ahead. The Golan, from where you could see across into Alsace. In front of it stood various cabins, with a foot and a half of snow on their roofs. Small trees were dotted here and there, their branches hanging low. He passed a wrapped palm and rose bushes weighed down by the snow. It was a mystical, dreamy, and suddenly dangerous winter wonderland.

He saw the light appear again, and this time it stayed on. It came from the cabin next to Ferati's plot. It was barely visible, the shutters were closed. He walked even more carefully now, making only slow progress.

Then he heard the sound. It travelled faintly through the night, but it was unmistakable. It was the miaowing of cats.

The door of the cabin was ajar. Hunkeler reached for the handle. Then he was struck hard on the head. He'd just caught a glimpse of something moving towards him, but didn't have time to dodge. It was a blow with a pole.

He went down, but remained conscious. Instinctively, he rolled to the left to evade a second clout. None came. The blow had hit home. He ran his hand across his hair. There was blood in it. A laceration, horribly painful. But his skull had withstood the impact. "Goddammit," he cursed and stood up. "Have you gone mad?"

Standing in the doorway was the man with the purple jacket and Borsalino hat. Next to him stood the pug-faced woman. The man had a rake in his hand. Neither of them said a word, they just stared at him anxiously.

"Are you completely crazy?" Hunkeler yelled. Then he remembered where he was. Besides, his head hurt too much to shout. "Are you nuts? What are you doing here?"

"*Grazie alla Madonna*," said the woman. "*No l'hai ucciso.* He's alive, you didn't kill him."

"I should hope so too," Hunkeler growled. "What were you thinking, lashing out with a rake like that?"

"*Scusi*," the man said with a soft, whiny voice. "I thought you were one of those intruders who go after foreigners. You're the Commissario, no?"

"Yes, I am. And who are you?"

"Rinaldi," the man said with a polite bow as he briefly lifted the hat off his head. "Rinaldi from Cremona. This is my wife Silvia. Please come in."

He stepped away from the door and Hunkeler entered. There were seven cats in the cabin, eating tinned food from a bowl. Four empty tins stood on the table, next to a gas lamp.

"Grappa?" Rinaldi asked.

"What do you mean, grappa? It's outrageous, hitting me over the head like that. And anyway, it's forbidden to enter the allotments. You know that perfectly well."

"The poor cats," the woman protested. "Who will feed them? Do you want them to starve?" She brought over a bottle of grappa.

"Yes, they can drop dead as far as I'm concerned," replied Hunkeler. "Close the door. Nobody needs to know we're here."

Rinaldi closed the door and fetched three shot glasses.

"Sit down," Silvia ordered.

Hunkeler complied. He could feel Silvia carefully checking the wound. "Ouch!" he called out. "What are you doing!"

"*Che brutto.* What a beast," she grumbled. "He would have struck you dead if I hadn't stepped in. *Un momento.*" She poured some schnapps over his hair.

"Ouch," he shouted again. "Are you trying to kill me?"

"*Salute*," said Rinaldi, and drained his glass.

"If you say so," muttered Hunkeler, and followed suit.

"I'm a poor roofer from Lombardy," said Rinaldi. "I can't work any more. I have a bad back. I live off a small pension and Silvia. I'm glad that I can stay in Switzerland."

Silvia nodded and refilled the glasses.

"The cats mean everything to me," Rinaldi continued. "They expect me every three days. They fill their bellies, then they go off somewhere to sleep. I can't just let them perish."

"Feeding cats is not allowed," Hunkeler snapped. "It says so in the allotment regulations."

"They aren't pets, they're strays. It's not my fault that they're here."

Silvia fished out a white bandage, which she probably intended to wrap around Hunkeler's head.

"*No grazie*," he said.

The cats had now polished off their food. All seven of them curled up on the bed, purring. A pennant for Inter Milan hung on one of the walls, below it an Adriano kit.

"Do you come here regularly?" Hunkeler asked.

"Whenever we can," Rinaldi replied. "We often spend the night here. It's quiet and the air is fresh."

"Shush," said Silvia, "you talk too much."

"Nonsense," Rinaldi protested. "He's a good man, he won't tell on us. We usually come into the allotments from Alsace, so nobody sees us. It's cosy here, even in winter." He pointed at the gas heater in the corner, the spirit burner, the packet soups on the shelf.

"Who set Ferati's cabin on fire?" Hunkeler asked him.

"I don't know. And I wouldn't tell you even if I did know. It would just cause trouble. It's best not to hear or see anything. There's always some quarrel or other going on in the allotments. There are always two groups at war with each other. Over nothing. But they always find a reason."

"And Ferati?"

"He's a proud man. Me, I don't get offended, but he does. I've told him to keep his head down, even when he's in the right. But he can't do that."

"Who killed the ducks?"

Rinaldi shook his head. "You won't get anything out of me."

"And if I lock you up because you hit me over the head?"

Rinaldi smiled politely. "You won't do that. You shouldn't be here either. *È vero?*"

"Yes, true. But I want to know who killed Flückiger. Did you sleep here on New Year's Night?"

"No," said Silvia.

"Yes," Rinaldi contradicted her. "We were here. There was lots of drinking and fireworks and the like. We didn't join in, we went to bed early."

"Toni Flückiger was murdered between two and three in the morning."

"We didn't notice anything unusual," said Silvia.

"We did," insisted Rinaldi. "I got woken at half two by someone creeping past our cabin. There were two young men, they had come over the Golan. They didn't want to be seen. But I saw them anyway."

"Where did they go?"

"They went in the direction of Flückiger's cabin."

"Sta zitto," his wife scolded. *"Che stupido,* you'll get us into trouble."

138

"And you? When did you leave your cabin?"

"We waited until everything went quiet," Rinaldi replied. "We were about to leave, but then the two young men came back. They moved very fast, then disappeared over the Golan. We were scared then, so we went home."

"Which route did you take?"

"The normal one, through the main entrance."

"Was it still snowing?"

"Yes," replied Rinaldi. "I think so."

"No," said his wife. "It had stopped. The path was covered with fresh snow. We were the first to leave any tracks in it. That was nice, as fresh and new as the new year."

"And now? Are you going to spend the night here?"

"No," said Rinaldi. "Or what do you think, Silvia?"

"*Ma sì*," she replied. "We will sleep here."

When Hunkeler was back in his car, he decided to spend the night in Basel. He had drunk three glasses of grappa. That was two too many for a night-time drive. And the wound on his head hurt. He prodded it, very carefully. He knew he wasn't good with pain. He noticed it had stopped bleeding.

And where was Hedwig now? Whenever he needed her, she was nowhere to be found. He longed for her gentle, dexterous fingers with which she would have examined the wound. For her consoling voice. It didn't bother her when he acted like a wimp. He reached for his phone and called her. He went through to voicemail. "Are you having a good time?" he asked. "I'm staying in Basel. A guy whacked me over the head. With a rake. I wish I was with you, so you could console me. But unfortunately that's not possible right now." He thought for a moment. "I'm coming to Colmar on Saturday. Or Sunday. I'd like to see the *Madonna of the Rose Garden* again. And you."

He set off towards town, but took a detour past the tyre warehouse. It wouldn't do for Haller to see him. He parked in front of the Luzernerring.

Cattaneo was sitting in an alcove at the back, with a glass of Armagnac. He didn't look up when Hunkeler sat down beside him, he seemed completely absorbed in himself.

"White coffee please," Hunkeler said to Mara when she came to the table. "And have a look at what's up with my head."

She carefully probed his hair. "It's lacerated," she observed. "It needs stitches really. But you'll survive without a doctor."

He waited a long time, quiet and calm like a cat in front of the mouse hole. He fetched some cigarettes from the machine, carefully tore open the packet and lit one up. "Aren't you watching the evening news today?" he asked.

Cattaneo didn't reply, it was as though he hadn't heard.

"Why were you in the allotments this evening? Why did you sneak through the hole in the fence? I saw the tracks of your rubber soles. Why were you in Flückiger's cabin on New Year's Eve? And when exactly? What did you talk to him about?"

"I've been waiting for you," said Cattaneo. "I don't know why. But I knew you would come."

140

"Four years is a long time," said Hunkeler. "Four long years to say goodbye and to recover. Or isn't that true?"

"You know it isn't true, otherwise you wouldn't be here," replied Cattaneo. He briefly glanced up and looked Hunkeler squarely in the eyes. He was clearly very depressed. He raised his glass and tipped the Armagnac down his throat. "Mara, another glass."

"You're drinking in memory of the deceased Toni Flückiger, aren't you?" Hunkeler observed.

"No, I'm drinking *with* the deceased Toni Flückiger. Four years is nothing. Time is nothing, in the face of death. There is only life and death. Death negates time. Death is far more real than life. Death is the only reality there is. I live in an illusionary world. Lucia lives in the real world, in the world of death. Toni Flückiger too. We're excluded from it, you and I. Because we're still alive."

"Are you drunk?" asked Hunkeler. "Is that why you have such dark thoughts?"

"Do I look drunk?"

"No, not really."

Mara brought another glass of Armagnac. "That's the last glass," she said. "The bottle is empty." She threw Hunkeler a worried look, but he didn't know what to do either.

"Watch you don't drink yourself to death," Hunkeler said. "For now, you're still alive. Death will come of its own accord sometime. There's no point waiting for it."

"I'm not waiting for it. It's waiting for me."

"You should go home and get some sleep, you're over-tired. Leave the past behind."

"I'm not at home anywhere. Not in the past either." Again he threw a brief, sharp look at Hunkeler. And again he drained the glass of Armagnac in one gulp. "Mara, a glass of cognac."

"Do you know who murdered Toni Flückiger?" Hunkeler asked him.

"No. If I knew, I'd kill him."

"You shouldn't do that. You need to leave it to us to punish the perpetrator."

"He was my wife's lover. I should have protected him from death. I didn't. I'm guilty."

"How did you find out?"

"She told me."

"Without you having asked?"

"Yes. The possibility had never occurred to me."

"So why did she tell you?"

"To protect herself. To protect our love, through her confession. Her confession helped her to free herself from Toni Flückiger. She didn't go back to him after she'd confessed. I only grasped this when she was dead. Not before, not even when she lay dying. But it was too late then." He shook his head, disgusted with the world, with himself, with his own stupidity. "It's terrible how time rules over everything. Over life, over love. We bumble along, as if we had eternity on our side. Then, from one second to the next, time dictates that it's all over. Finish, the end. The dreadful thing is that there's a beginning and an end. The end is final. All that's left is the past, memories. But even the past is determined by time. Until finally death comes and dissolves the past."

"You've developed an entire philosophy," commented Hunkeler. "I hope it helps you."

"No, it doesn't help me. It plunges me into despair. Do you know what despair originally meant? It meant the unknown. We all live in the unknown, all our lives. Death is our home."

Hunkeler was silent. Where did the man get these ideas from? "You're a laboratory assistant, aren't you?" he asked. "What does that mean exactly? What does a laboratory assistant do?"

"He works in the chemical industry. I did the same work as a technician, but for lower pay. Because I didn't do an apprenticeship. Because I'm a wop from the Aosta Valley. But I've read books all my life. Nietzsche and Jaspers and the like. The problem is, I didn't apply what I read to myself, to my own life. I only tried after Lucia died. It was too late then."

"Come now, stop wallowing in these gloomy thoughts," said Hunkeler. "Life goes on. It's never too late to change."

"What use is it if I change now? I can't change what's happened. And I can't accept it either. I can't accept my guilt. Nor do I believe in forgiveness, I'm not a Christian."

"If you've read Nietzsche, you should forget about the notion of guilt." Hunkeler hesitated for a while, then decided to say it. "I think Lucia has long forgiven you."

"That's possible. But I can't forgive myself."

"And what criteria is that based on? Guilt is a thoroughly Christian concept. If you're not a Christian, you shouldn't speak of guilt."

"Are you trying to lecture me, huh, copper?" A hint of scorn flashed up in Cattaneo's eyes. "I don't need that. If I want to pronounce myself guilty, then I will. Whether you like it or not." He reached for the cognac Mara had brought. "I destroyed Lucia's life. In doing it, I also destroyed my life without realizing it. She tried everything to make our love work. She sought to seduce me with love. And she often

143

succeeded, briefly at least. Those moments were wonderful, I'm grateful to her for that. But then came her confession. I couldn't accept it for what it was, a declaration of love. I was too much of a fool to understand. I didn't do the right thing."

"What would have been the right thing?"

"I should have forgiven her," replied Cattaneo. He sat there, immobile and deathly pale. Then two tears rolled down his cheeks. They remained hanging there, he didn't wipe them away. "I should have shown mercy, compassion. Instead, I was cruel, unloving, cold-hearted. I never touched her again, I punished her. Have you ever experienced someone very close to you dying of cancer?"

"No."

"It's a slow, horrific, steadily increasing obliteration. The fact that Lucia had to die, I could have borne that perhaps. But not this degrading obliteration."

"What did she say about it?"

"Nothing. We didn't talk about it. She died without a word. And I watched without a word."

"I know people who have lost their loved ones to cancer," said Hunkeler. "They're all scarred, they all feel guilty."

"She died like an angel, life floated out of her body. She left me behind in hell. She turned me into a devil." More tears spilled from his eyes. He wiped them away. "Why am I telling you all of this? Do you know?"

"Perhaps because you shot Toni Flückiger," replied Hunkeler. "You have two possible motives. The first is simple. Toni Flückiger intruded into your relationship. After everything I've heard, it's clear you must have loved each other."

"What have you heard?"

"That Lucia was a happy, vivacious woman. She must have had a reason to stay with you. That reason could only have been love."

"And what would the second motive be?"

"The second motive is quite obscure. Going by what you've said, you're longing for death because death is the essence and life is just a precursor to it."

"That's right. We're destined to die."

"You blame yourself because you didn't forgive Lucia. Complete forgiveness would have meant stepping aside and giving your blessing to her new love."

"What gives you that idea?" asked Cattaneo, his eyes flaring.

"You said as much yourself, I'm just spelling it out. You're suffering under your assumed guilt. You want to rid yourself of this guilt. The best way you can do this is to reunite Lucia with Toni Flückiger. And as Lucia is dead, this can only be done through death. Therefore, it's possible that you killed Toni Flückiger to bring him and Lucia together again."

"True, it's possible," said Cattaneo. Some of the colour had come back to his face. The conversation seemed to enliven him. "And if I had done it, how would I have gone about it? Where would I have got hold of a gun, for example?"

"You can buy a gun in any small-arms shop."

"And how would I have managed to hang him from the meathook?"

"You would have found yourself in exceptional circumstances. In such situations people are much stronger."

"So I would have achieved something in my dismal life after all, would you say?"

"Yes," Hunkeler replied. "That's how it could have happened."

"Do you want to arrest me? I would willingly come."

"No."

"Why not?"

"Because I have no proof."

"So you want me to confess. You're too stupid to realize I've just provided a full confession. I killed my wife. But not the way you mean. You're a simple soul, Inspector. You need verifiable crimes. Shooting, beating, strangling someone. But real crimes are of a different nature. If you want to arrest me for heartlessness, for the inability to empathize, then do so. I'd have no objection to coming with you. But I guess that doesn't fit into your ludicrous world of rules and regulations." He threw another sharp look at Hunkeler, this time steady and confident. Again there was a hint of scorn in it.

Hunkeler got up and left.

He drove slowly past Kannenfeld Park. The last number 3 tram towards the border passed by, its green carriages shimmering in the night-time glow. The outlines of the snow-laden trees stood out sharply against the clear sky. It was a bright, magical night.

He parked the car outside his apartment. He didn't feel like going up, even though the conversation with Cattaneo had worn him out and his head still hurt. He took out his phone and called Hedwig.

"Yes?" she whispered.

"It's me, Peter. Where are you?"

"At the Hotel Le Maréchal in Colmar, in bed. Do you know what time it is?"

"Yes. It's a magical night."

She yawned, she must have been asleep already. "How's your head?"

"Not good," he replied. "I'm not doing too well."

"Why do you always have to get into a fight? You know you're an old man now."

"I didn't get into a fight," he barked. "I was attacked. Do you love me?"

"I think you're losing it. You know full well that I love you."

"Even when I'm unkind to you?"

"Listen, I want to sleep now," she told him. "I'm tired. And I would never love an unkind man. Good night."

He got out of the car and walked up the street to St Johanns-Ring. The fountain on the corner was frozen over and the water trickled down cascades of ice into the basin. He followed the narrow path that people had trodden into the snow. A car drove past, with open windows. A loudspeaker was blasting Arabic rap into the night. The Sommereck was closed. Edi was probably lying in bed snoring.

Was it Cattaneo who had killed Flückiger? Should he have taken him in to the Waaghof? Lock him up, harass him a bit, wait for him to lose his cool? No, that wouldn't get them anywhere. Assuming he'd done it, Cattaneo would simply withdraw into his own obscure world, thereby immunizing himself. Perhaps he would have been glad to come, because he needed an audience for his agonized self-incrimination.

Perhaps he was thinking of killing himself in one of the coming nights. It was possible, but Hunkeler didn't think so. The confession had been a little too self-pitying, too corny. He would never have confessed to a real murder.

He saw an animal dart across the road. He glimpsed its bright winter coat, its elongated, beautiful wild movement. It jumped across the banked snow that separated the sidewalk from the road and disappeared into a driveway. A marten, out on its nightly hunt.

Burgfelderplatz was peaceful and quiet. He briefly looked across to the sex shop, the shopping centre, the pharmacy. The distant sound of wheels turning on tracks carried across from the direction of the border. It was the number 3 tram, heading back into the city.

He entered the Milchhüsli. Hauser stood at the bar with a glass of schnapps in front of him. "Come here," he said. "Join me for a drink."

Hunkeler ordered a beer.

"So, how's business?" Hauser asked.

"You bastard," said Hunkeler. "I'm going to punch your lights out one day, you just wait."

"Go ahead, don't be shy," Hauser replied. "We all know I'm the scum of the earth."

Hunkeler looked over to the billiard players. The gardener from Aargau was also in his spot, like every evening.

"What are you doing here, anyway?"

"Where else should I be?" Hauser asked.

"In the Emmental, I'd have thought. In Rüegsbach."

Hauser downed his schnapps and ordered another. "You're my guest this evening," he said. "The drinks are on me. Do you know what Toni Flückiger's real name was?"

"No."

"Yes you do, I can see it in your face. You were right to become a police officer. You're no good at lying. A reporter has to know how to lie through their teeth. A reporter has to be a pig, the kind that's happy to wallow in the vilest muck. That's me, I'm good at that. But there are even bigger swines. Like the ones in Zurich. If you live in Basel, you don't stand a chance against them."

"What's happened?"

"They've taken the Flückiger story off me."

"But you were the one who hit on it and made it into something."

"They want to make it into something even bigger. They left for Rüegsbach at lunchtime today, with an entire team of people. Without Hauser. He's too stupid for them."

He was near to tears, poor fat Hauser. He was cut to the quick.

"Take a look at the papers tomorrow. You'll get to read a great big sob story. About the stubborn, heartless Emmental people. About the oppression of a loving woman. About the persecution of a noble, brave Russian who managed to escape into Switzerland by the skin of his teeth. More schmaltz than you can imagine. It makes me want to puke."

"Why a Russian?" Hunkeler asked.

"Because they say Toni Flückiger was Russian. Why do you ask?"

"No reason. I reckon Toni Flückiger was from East Prussia."

"Is that certain?"

"Nothing is certain. How did you find out about the fake passport?"

"We have our sources. We don't name them, you know that. The only thing we don't have yet is the real name. Even the greedy pigs in Zurich don't have it. It seems there's a code of silence on that in Rüegsbach. Nothing to be done."

He glanced sideways at Hunkeler, devious, sly, alert. "Do you have the name?"

"I've already told you, no."

"The chief editor told me to get the lowdown about what's happening in Basel. Said I should fish around in the cesspool of the allotments. Shine a light on those castles of kitsch, the yearnings they represent, the repressed passions of the petit bourgeois. Stories, pictures, the works. I can't be bothered with all that. I'm not going to do it, end of story. I don't give a shit who killed four ducks and fourteen rabbits."

"But animal stories are always a winner, aren't they?"

"I'm sick to the back teeth of it. Imagine you're onto a really big story. A brutal murder, a dark, mysterious figure, everything taking place on the border between Basel and Alsace, with connections back to the Second World War. And then they take it all away from you." Another sly sideways glance. "If I had the real name, I might be able to get the story back again."

"Sorry," said Hunkeler. "I can't help you. Thanks for the beer."

When Hunkeler walked into the Sommereck the following morning at nine, Edi was sitting at a table with a glass of water in front of him, mixing a white powder into it.

"See what I have to suffer," he grumbled. "Soon all I'll be allowed to eat is chalk, like the wolf in the Grimms' fairy tale of the seven young goats. What do I have left to live for?"

"The satisfaction of bringing me a coffee," replied Hunkeler and reached for the tabloid.

"Didn't you get round to combing your hair this morning?" Edi asked.

"Couldn't. Somebody whacked me over the head."

"My God, the things you get up to."

The title page carried a nice headline: "Three roses for Sonja". Next to it was a photo of Sonja Flückiger, who had been given a thorough going-over by a hairdresser. Freshly blow-dried, her face powdered and made up, she was looking at the camera full of bewilderment. Pages two and three were entirely dedicated to the old woman from the Emmental who had loved and taken in a poor Russian. But the village elders hadn't approved of this. Full of spite, they had chased the Russian away to Basel, where he was later killed. The brave Sonja was put under huge pressure and was left to waste away on water and bread. Even her electricity had been cut. The son she'd had with the Russian was driven away to Zurich, where he died, a victim of the open drug scene on Platzspitz. Only old Fritz from Hinterglatt still looked out for Sonja. He brought her free wood and potatoes. Despite the cruel oppression, the valiant, faithful woman had remained steadfast and had not given away the Russian's name and origins. In fidelity, faith and defiance – these her own words – she had held out and defied the village chiefs. And to this day she had kept safe her most cherished treasure, a present from the Russian. It was three paper roses, which he had won for her at a shooting stall at the Sumiswald fair. Question: *What secret is Sonja hiding?* Answer: *Watch this space.*

Hunkeler looked at the large photo on page two. Everything was there that he'd seen on his visit. Cupboard, table, coffee pot, sugar tin. Only the three roses were different. They had put new ones on the table.

He briefly leafed through the *Basler Zeitung* to see whether they had anything about Livius. There was a short piece, stating that Anton Flückiger could not be the same person as Livius, as Livius had been killed in action in Russia. The investigation was being conducted with every available resource.

Hunkeler reached for the tabloid again and looked at it closely. Something was missing. It took him a while to work out what. Then he realized. The mouse was missing.

The bottom right-hand corner of page three was given over to a charity appeal for Sonja Flückiger. That cheered Hunkeler up. "So, at least one good thing will come from this pig's ear of an investigation," he said.

"Talking of pigs," Edi piped up, "I have this home-made liver sausage from the Black Forest. An absolute revelation with fresh bread and pickled gherkins."

"Well bring it out then," said Hunkeler. "Let's dig in."

When he left, Hunkeler walked along Mittlere Strasse to Kannenfeld Park. He needed to move, his back had become stiff during the night. He ought to call the chiropractor to see whether they could fit him in, he thought. They generally found the time to lay him on the table and loosen his compacted vertebrae with a short, precise tug.

But Hunkeler didn't want to. Now was not the time to think about his back. Now was the time to lie in ambush, waiting for the moment when the truth revealed itself. And that moment, he was sure, was very close.

He passed Cattaneo's house. It was a hundred-year-old stone building, two-storey, terraced like all houses on this road. A yew stood in the front garden, its branches forced down over the iron fence by the snow. There was a copper bell button, with ETTORE CATTANEO engraved into the plate. It was a proud name for the man from the Aosta Valley, a proud house for a laboratory assistant with no apprenticeship.

He was a strange chap, this Cattaneo. A philosopher who must have spent entire nights reading. Who had developed his own theory about time and eternity. Hunkeler had understood where he was coming from. He too suffered under the absoluteness of the past. He too wished he had acted differently in some important situations in his life. But he'd come to terms with the fact that things had happened the way they had happened. And he knew where he came from. A rural, lower-middle-class family that had never learned to make active decisions and deal with things. Instead, they had let decisive situations come towards them until they could no longer be changed.

That was probably how it had been with Cattaneo. Until he had no other choice but to watch wordlessly while his wife died without a word. Only then, when he was looking at the cancer-ravaged corpse, was he roused from his lethargy.

Was it then, four years ago, that he'd resolved to take action? Had he decided not to shoulder all the blame for his wife's death but to apportion some of it to Toni Flückiger? Had he finally punished him on that New Year's Eve? The idea seemed fanciful. And yet Hunkeler couldn't rid himself of it. He wondered whether he should ring the bell, go and talk to the man. He decided to let it be, it was too soon.

He crossed the road to the park. To his right stood the handsome old cafe Zur Entenweid. It was up for sale, according to the notice. The landlord had given up six months ago, it hadn't made enough money. The adjoining kiosk, where he used to sell cigarettes and newspapers, was also closed. Nobody spent any money round here, it was a pointless part of town.

A high-speed train came racing out of the tunnel that led under the crossing and through to Alsace. He could see the pantographs of the locomotive sliding along the overhead line. The pale roofs of the wagons. Then the red light, disappearing around a bend.

Hunkeler entered the park. He followed in the tracks the joggers had put down. He didn't run a single yard, his back wasn't up to it. Instead he walked fast, made sure to breathe deeply in and out. On several occasions, younger people overtook him. Some older men also jogged past. He didn't care.

He did two laps, then went into Erkan's cafe and ordered a mineral water. Gazing through the window, he watched some kids as they sledged down a small hill. It was still freezing cold out there. A girl burst into tears and stuck her red, raw fingers into her mouth. Another decisively sat herself on a wooden sledge and raced straight into two boys who were crawling up the slope. All of them were wrapped up in red, yellow and blue polar jackets. Life in all its colours, he thought.

The writer was standing at the bar. Hunkeler hadn't noticed him at first. He came over to Hunkeler's table. "I must thank you," he said. "You provided me with the solution to my problem."

"Glad to hear it," Hunkeler replied. "And what solution is this?"

"The solution is the Viagra. So, my story goes like this: Flückiger seduces Lucia. Cattaneo doesn't realize, the possibility never occurs to him. Lucia tells him, she confesses. She wants to free herself from Flückiger. She loves Cattaneo and wants to stay with him. Cattaneo feels deeply insulted. Instead of fighting for Lucia, he becomes cold and distant. He lets Lucia languish until she dies. Then he decides to kill Flückiger. Are you following me?"

"Yes, I am. What I don't like about your story is the woman's role. Doesn't Lucia get to make any decisions?"

"No," said the writer, and he seemed very sure about this. "The woman is the victim. She is ground down by the two men. Her only chance is to stay with Flückiger. But no woman can stay with him. She knows that."

Outside, Cattaneo appeared, with Giovanna trailing two yards behind. They entered the cafe and sat down without speaking to each other.

"So far, it's a totally standard crime plot," the writer continued. "Used countless times, for example by Simenon. The familiar triangle of husband, wife and seducer. It always ends the same. The wife wants to stay with her husband, but he no longer wants her. And the seducer no longer wants her either. That's why the wife is in the victim's role."

"The story could also be interpreted differently," Hunkeler commented. "And we shouldn't talk so loudly. He might hear us."

"Don't worry, he isn't listening. He isn't even looking at his new girlfriend. He's completely caught up in himself."

Giovanna glanced up and stared over at them with venomous eyes.

"She's a nobody," the writer commented. "She follows him around like a dog. The new, brilliant thing about my story is that the husband doesn't simply gun down the seducer. Instead, he sets out to humiliate and torment him. He sits down with him under the pretence of seeking a reconciliation. That gives him the opportunity to secretly mix an overdose of Viagra into the drink. Soon, the seducer has an erection he can't get rid of. It's so strong he almost explodes, and he dies of a heart attack. I bet you haven't read anything like that yet. I'm the first to come up with it."

"That's a revolting story," replied Hunkeler.

Giovanna stood up and approached their table, stony-faced, anger flashing in her eyes. "You aren't a writer," she said. "You're a stupid idiot." Then she walked out.

Surprised, the writer watched her go. Then his eyes narrowed to slits that flashed with a steely pride. "See?" he said. "I was spot on. This is the first time she's ever said anything to me."

Cattaneo hadn't moved an inch. He sat there motionless with both hands on the table, between them the untouched cup of coffee.

"I think she's right," remarked Hunkeler and stood up.

Outside, he saw Giovanna striding down the path with determination. She didn't look back, she'd probably had enough, once and for all. Isn't it odd, Hunkeler thought, how life drives people to form the most unlikely relationships, just to escape the horror of loneliness. As so often, he felt thankful he had Hedwig.

On the nearby slope, a woman wrapped in dark garments and a headscarf set about sledging down the hill with two kids. The children were clad in red plastic outfits, he couldn't tell whether boy or girl. The woman had placed them in front of her on the sledge. Sitting at the back, she pushed off with her feet. They gained speed and narrowly missed a mother who was pulling her whining son up the hill. The trio only came to a halt when they hit another sledge that was positioned crosswise and had two girls sitting on it eating ice cream bought at Erkan's kiosk.

Hunkeler walked across the park. He wasn't sure what to do. He knew he should probably drive to the Waaghof and study the files that were most likely piling up on his desk. But he didn't feel like it. He sat down on a stone sculpture of a sea lion and called Lüdi.

"Yes?"

"Hunkeler here. Any news from Potsdam?"

"No, nothing from Potsdam. They don't seem to have any more information on Russius after Carlsbad."

"Surely that's not possible."

"Apparently it is. It seems he vanished into thin air."

Hunkeler heard Lüdi chuckle quietly, almost gloatingly. "What is it?" he asked.

"Dogan has confessed to torching Ferati's cabin."

"For God's sake. Why?"

"No idea. I don't really get it. They seem to belong to different Islamic denominations. Who'd have known?"

"The Battle of Villmergen, 1712," said Hunkeler.

"Pardon?"

"Villmergen in Aargau. That's where the Swiss Catholics and Swiss Protestants came to blows with each other for the last time. That was in 1712, less than three hundred years ago."

"Stop talking nonsense."

"It's not nonsense. It's a documented fact."

"If you say so. You can give us a lecture on it at the 4 p.m. briefing."

"I won't be there," replied Hunkeler.

"What?"

"Sorry. I'm driving back to Alsace. I'm exempt from work, special tasks only, remember? I'll call you later this evening."

"I have a date with my boyfriend," Lüdi told him a little sheepishly.

"I have your private number, darling."

Hunkeler left the park and walked down Mülhauserstrasse towards the Rhine. He passed the Nordbahnhof, the only bar in the St Johann quarter that hadn't been turned into a pizzeria, a Turkish cafe or a kebab house in recent years. Nor had it been repurposed as a pharmacy or bank branch. It had remained a local bar. That had only been possible because the carnival clique that held its meetings there had decided to acquire the property. Once again, Hunkeler praised the power and ingenuity afforded by money.

He crossed Elsässerstrasse and reached the Rhine. He had thought of visiting the St Johann bathhouse further along. He had the key for it in his pocket. But now he stopped and looked across the river, up to the Johanniter and Mittlere bridges and the Minster above. The low winter sun fell obliquely on the water's surface. Three cormorants cut across the river, like three black crosses. A swan glided along the bank, unbelievably white. Hunkeler turned and walked back to Elsässerstrasse. He had decided to pay someone a visit.

Dogan lived in a cheap 1950s apartment block. Tattered bikes stood on the front lawn, among them a trailer with flat tyres and a rocking horse that had lost its head. There was also a spanking clean road bike that presumably belonged to a keen cyclist.

Hunkeler rang the bell several times before the entrance door sprung open. He climbed four flights of stairs. A young woman with a headscarf stood in the open doorway. "Hello," he greeted her. "Please don't be worried. My name is Hunkeler and I'm from the police. I just want to talk to you for a minute. Are you Dilara Dogan?"

She didn't move, just nodded.

"It's freezing out there," he continued. "Would you mind making me a coffee?"

She turned and walked along the hallway into the kitchen.

He followed her and sat down at the kitchen table. He would have liked to smoke, but he didn't want to take liberties.

Dilara stood with her back to the stove and gazed at him. She was very pale, she probably hadn't slept much.

"I know your father is in custody," he said. "I'm assuming he'll be released soon. What I'd like to know is, why did your father dislike Toni Flückiger?"

"Is he going to be deported?" she asked.

Hunkeler didn't know. "I don't think so," he finally said. "What's your situation?"

"I'm going to get married, next March. My fiancé is of Turkish descent, but he has Swiss citizenship." She was still looking at him without moving.

"You go to college, don't you?"

"Yes, Leonhard College on Barfüsserplatz. My father didn't dislike Toni Flückiger. He barely knew him. You're welcome to smoke, if you want." She placed an ashtray on the

159

table, then she poured ground coffee and sugar into a little copper pot, filled it with water and set it down on the stove. She did it slowly and gracefully, and he enjoyed watching her. "It's ancient business, I don't want to have anything to do with that stuff," she said. "I'm a committed Muslim, my husband-to-be is a Christian. We love each other and I firmly believe we will have a happy family. My father disapproves of it. There's a lot he disapproves of. The same with Herr Ferati. The two of them are fighting a battle that was lost a long time ago. It makes me so sad I can barely sleep." The coffee on the stove came to the boil. She poured it into a little cup and handed it to Hunkeler.

He thanked her and tried to take a sip, but the coffee was too hot. He lit a cigarette instead.

"The fact that he got locked up doesn't worry me much," she continued. "Perhaps he'll finally realize that the laws here are different. I want to love and honour my father. It's very difficult sometimes."

"He probably won't be allowed to keep the allotment," Hunkeler said between sips. He loved Turkish coffee. He loved the poster on the wall depicting the Hagia Sophia. He loved the wall hanging with the Arabic *surah* that he couldn't read.

"My father grew up on Lake Van, in the east, close to the Iraq border. He's a committed Kurd, he yearns for Kurdistan. There's a lot I can't talk to him about. He still dreams of me returning to his village with him. I'm not going to do that. I'm going to take on his allotment."

"Welcome to Basel," he said.

She looked at him, surprised. "Stop with that crap," she snapped.

"Sorry. I didn't mean to offend you."

"Just cut out the rubbish. Why are you here, anyway?"

"Because I wanted to talk to you."

"Well, you've done that. And you've had coffee too. So?"

"Who killed the rabbits? And the ducks?"

"How am I supposed to know? Anything else?"

"Not really," he replied and stubbed out his cigarette.

"I don't need your sympathy," she told him. "Now go please."

He stood up and went to the door. She was already holding it open for him. He wanted to say goodbye, but couldn't think of anything suitable to say, so he just gave a hint of a bow. She laughed, she probably found him quaint. "You're a funny one," she said. "They should put you in a museum."

As Hunkeler drove towards the border, he recalled Dilara laughing at him. He'd behaved like an utter idiot. She was right, they should put him in a museum. But first he had to take care of something.

Haller and his Alsatian colleague were standing by the entrance to the allotments. Hunkeler lowered his window. He noticed that the compressor had gone silent. "What's up? Why have they switched the compressor off?"

"No idea," Haller replied. "They don't tell us anything."

"Has anyone tried to get into the allotments?"

"No, it's all been quiet. Aren't you going to the briefing?"

"No, not today. Go steady. And keep your eyes peeled."

He drove along the Hohe Strasse. The sun was a red ball hanging low over the western horizon, set in a sky of steely grey. At the top, by Trois Maisons, you could see far into the Vosges mountains.

He turned off towards his village. There was still lots of snow on the road up here. When he reached the St Imbert cross, he got out. Someone had placed three paper flowers in front of it, red carnations. Who had done that? A huntsman, or a child? He would have liked to cross himself, but he didn't know how, so he let it be.

He parked outside his house, fetched the snow shovel and cleared the area in front of the door. He lit a fire in the kitchen stove and in the front room and fed the two cats. Then he went into the barn to chop some wood. He struck the axe into a piece of beechwood and lifted it high above his head to smack it down onto the chopping block. But then the pain shot through his back again. "Ouch!" he shouted. "Damn it."

It made him livid every time he experienced that pain. As far as he was concerned, his back's job was to function as expected, that's what it was there for. He went to fetch some painkillers from the kitchen and washed them down with a glass of water. Then he watched the hens through the window as they scraped clear a section of ground under the willow. They were bustling about, pecking and scratching, even though there clearly wasn't much to peck at in this cold. At one point Fritz the cockerel tried to mount one of the hens. He gripped her by the small comb, spread his clipped wings wide and gave a brief, hoarse crow. The hen wasn't interested and shook him off. It was probably too cold.

A female chaffinch flew onto the windowsill and looked in. Hunkeler fetched bird food, carefully opened the window and sprinkled some onto the sill. The bird waited a while, then hopped over and pecked at the crumbs.

The sun had set and dusk slowly enveloped the house. He left the kitchen light off and watched the transformation with keen interest. Bit by bit, the wall of the pigsty next to the pear tree dissolved into the dark. The thick trunk of the willow appeared to blacken and sink away, then the snow began to gleam as if a distinct light source dwelled within it. The entire garden seemed to glow beneath the black sky, where the first stars now appeared.

He went outside to let the hens in. He opened the hen-house door, scattered grain onto the floor and called out "Here, chuck chuck chuck." This wasn't necessary, the hens would have come running anyway. He called to them purely out of habit, and also because he liked doing it. Then he set about delivering a speech to Fritz the cockerel. "You've got it made," he said. "You're the cock of the roost here. All you have to do is scratch around in the ground and eat, crow in the morning and hop onto one of your nine lady friends every now and then, provided it isn't too cold. You get your food delivered free of charge and you don't even have to lay eggs. But what about me, weary, burned-out old bird that I am. I scratch and scratch around all day and all evening until gone midnight without finding even the tiniest worm. If I ever crow a bit too loudly, I get a smack round the head. And regarding women, there's no way I could ever achieve your quota. I'm just glad when my only woman occasionally claims to be satisfied with me."

He closed up the henhouse, walked through the barn and across the road, and went into the neighbour's cowshed.

There were only two cows left there now, plus a year-ling and two calves. He could hear the pigs squealing in the back.

The farmer's wife was milking the cows and feeding the milk to the calves and pigs. There was no drop-off point for milk in the village any more. The area had been given over to maize cultivation, which was ruining the soil and the groundwater.

Hunkeler sat down on the bench by the wall and stroked the dog that had come wagging over to him. "Where's the farmer?" he asked, even though he knew where he was.

"At the inn," the woman replied. "Playing skat."

"Thank you for looking after the hens," he said.

"You're welcome. But you'll have to get a new cockerel. *Il est trop vieux*, he's not going to last much longer." She was trying to coax one of the calves into drinking. She pushed the teat into its mouth but the animal refused, so she tried again with her fingers. This worked. She quickly shoved the teat in and the calf drank.

"Who picked up the badger?" Hunkeler asked.

"Edmond, he's a huntsman. He rendered down the fat. It's good against *le rheumatisme*."

"Who put the flowers there?"

"I don't know." She took the empty bucket away and refilled it to feed the other calf. "He can't bear it that he's not allowed to be a proper farmer any more," she said. "Just the maize. He's not happy about that. He doesn't want to poison the ground he inherited." She went over to the second calf and used both fingers again. It worked with this one too, the animal greedily gulped down the milk. "I read the report in the *Alsace*, about the allotments on the

164

border," she told him. "It said they hung up a man with a meathook. How can anyone do such a thing?"

"I don't know."

"I read that the Police Nationale is in charge."

"I'm working alongside them," he told her.

"And you don't know?"

Hunkeler was instantly alert. "What don't I know?"

"It's an old story. People don't like to talk about it. We try to forget. But still we remember. *On n'oublie pas.*"

Hunkeler ran his hand across the dog's head, slowly and affectionately, as if he was fond of him. The animal grunted with pleasure.

"I immediately thought of it when I read about the business with the meathook," she said. "I mean, who would come up with such an idea? Like a dead animal, strung up like a pig. No normal person would do that."

He agreed with her, those had been his thoughts too.

"I don't even know whether it truly happened that way," she told him as she removed the empty bucket to refill it for the pigs. "I know the German soldiers were poor bastards too, just like us Alsatians. They also had to obey. *Mais quandmême*, that went too far."

She carried the milk pail to the pigsty at the back. The dog whined briefly but stayed behind, his nose was too delicate. Hunkeler watched as the woman poured the milk into the trough. The three pigs sloshed the milk about with their snouts.

"I'm not familiar with the story," Hunkeler said. "But it seems to me that I ought to be."

"What's definite is that all young Alsatians were conscripted in February 1943," she continued. "They were going to be sent to the Eastern Front. Everybody knew that. My husband was conscripted too, he was eighteen at the time. He was taken to the barracks at Karlsruhe. There they said to him: 'Right, you back-country dimwit. We're going to make a proper human out of you now!' I didn't know him yet back then, but he's told me about it several times."

She laughed briefly and shook her head. She had put the empty bucket down in front of her and they both watched as the pigs guzzled the milk.

"Shortly before they were due to be transported to the Eastern Front, he escaped. A German truck driver hid him and took him over the Rhine bridge back into Alsace. He ran all through the night. When he arrived home, his parents were scared. He was going to be shot if they caught him, and they would become forced labourers somewhere in Germany. They hid him until the first French tanks came rolling in."

She carried the bucket back into the cowshed and switched off the milking machine. Hunkeler sat back down, he wanted to hear more.

The woman paused, wondering whether she should carry on talking. "Many terrible things happened during that time," she said. "People today don't understand. I don't like to speak ill of the Germans. *On est des amis, n'est-ce pas?* We're on friendly terms. And we still talk in our German dialect, at least us old folks do. They were classed as deserters, the young lads. That's what happens when there's a war. There were eighteen of them, from the Ballersdorf area. They tried to flee to Switzerland, via Seppois and through the forest. There used to be a railway line along there, it's been dismantled since. They ran into a German patrol. One of the lads had a gun. He fired it at a German soldier, who died the following day. He shouldn't have done that. *Mais qu'est-ce qu'on veut*, Monsieur? What can one say? You can understand why, can't you?"

Hunkeler nodded. Yes, he understood.

"Three of the lads were shot dead, one escaped. He ran to the nearest farm and asked to be taken in. They chased him away, they were too scared of the SS. He ran to another farm. They chased him away too. He ran to a third farm. There they took him in and hid him. The SS searched the entire farmstead, but they didn't find him. He escaped to Switzerland later on."

She stood there, motionless. She was at pains to recount events accurately.

"The other fourteen ran home and hid. They were picked up the following morning and shot. People say their bodies were hung up with meathooks as a deterrent."

The woman briefly laughed again. It was a very sad laugh.

"Thankfully I've never heard anyone say that they strung up the lads alive. At least that. They shot them first. Otherwise we'd never be able to forgive them. Even so, it's difficult enough *de pardonner*. But a time has to come when things are put to rest, *n'est-ce pas?*"

Hunkeler chugged along the softly undulating road to Knoeringue. Not for the first time, he was amazed at his own ignorance, his naivety. He'd known the farmer's wife for over twenty years, and he knew the farmer quite well too. He liked living in Alsace. Not always, he liked

Basel too. But he loved the tranquillity here, the leisurely pace at which people did things. He felt a fondness for the area.

He had a general idea of what had happened in Alsace during the two world wars. How the men had had to change uniforms multiple times and had no choice in the matter. He had visited Struthof once, years ago. The former concentration camp had made him feel so depressed he'd sworn never to go there again. He also knew about the 130,000 men from Alsace-Lorraine, the *Malgré-nous*, who were sent to the Eastern Front, where 40,000 of them died. But he had never heard anyone speak about it.

He parked in front of the Scholler family's inn. There were only three cars out front. The road was too icy for the day trippers from Basel.

He stepped inside and went across to old Frau Scholler, who was sitting at the family table in the back corner. "May I?"

"*Mais bien sûr*, Monsieur. Take a seat. Have you eaten yet?"

Dinner was bread soup with cumin, followed by stuffed cabbage rolls, boiled potatoes and salad, with a glass of wine.

"To what do I owe this pleasure?" she asked.

"My hunger. And my curiosity."

She laughed. At nearly eighty, she was still full of the joys of spring. She told him about one of her grandsons, who was recovering from the measles. About old Jeannot, who had cycled home a couple of days ago and fallen off his bike on the bend, because of the ice. About the big white dog, who used to bark at every guest who walked through the door but now spent all day lying in the kitchen, sleeping.

"And how are you? What's your lady up to?"

"She's in Colmar, with a girlfriend," he told her. "They've gone to see the Isenheim Altarpiece."

"But you will go and visit her?"

"Yes, when my work is done and I have time."

"Of course, you're probably busy with that murder case," she said.

He nodded and cut into one of the cabbage rolls which Babette had brought out. They were a bit over-salted, a bit too greasy. He topped up his wine glass from the bottle.

"Who would do a thing like that?" she wondered. "Who would hang a dead man up with a hook?"

"What happened back then, in Ballersdorf?" he asked.

"Yes, I thought of Ballersdorf straight away when I read about it in the paper. Turn the radio down, Babette," she called across into the kitchen. "The music isn't suitable." The radio was turned down. It was tuned to Südwestrundfunk 4, some jolly Tyrolean chaps were on.

"First they shot them in the knees, so they couldn't run away again. Then they hung them up alive with meathooks. Whether that's true, I don't know. That's what I heard. Although I cannot imagine how anybody on God's earth could do such a thing. *Mais qu'est-ce qu'on veut, Monsieur?* What can one say? It's what war does to people. It turns them into animals."

"And you, how did you experience the war?"

"It was bad enough. We were evacuated before the war had even properly started. That was on 1 September 1939. We were taken to Les Landes on the Atlantic. We didn't know if we could ever return. The people from your village were allowed to stay in their homes, they didn't belong to the Saint-Louis district. But we were within the border region."

"When did you come back?"

"After France had capitulated and Pétain ruled. My mother got by somehow. We weren't too badly off, the Germans liked to come and drink a beer at our inn. Just one thing bothered me. I was christened Jeanne. Then suddenly I was supposed to be called Johanna. Luckily I also have a middle name, Edith. So my mother simply called me Edith from then on. They were satisfied with that."

Hunkeler now tucked into the apple tart Babette had brought him.

"There was this sergeant at the company headquarters," Frau Scholler continued. "My mother was on friendly terms with him. We had six cows that were registered. They kept strict records on this, we had to hand over every single litre of milk. But we also had a seventh cow. That one wasn't registered. Every time the inspection officer was on his way, this sergeant would call and say a thunderstorm was approaching. Me and my sister would run off into the woods with the cow until the coast was clear again. You know, Monsieur, the Germans are not worse than the French. We Alsatians were just unlucky to be living between Germany and France. Really, we're neither German nor French, we're Alsatian. We speak our own dialect, just like you do, *n'est-ce pas?* During the German occupation we weren't allowed to speak a single word of French. Then, after the war, we weren't allowed to speak Alsatian during school break time."

"Is it true about them being shot in the knees?" Hunkeler asked.

"I'm just telling you what I've heard. Perhaps people pictured it being like that to express the terror. It's Friday tomorrow. Come by at midday. Konrad Rinser comes for

170

lunch every Friday. He also escaped to Switzerland back then. He's ninety, he knows about it."

"Thank you, I will. Do you have any Armagnac?"

"*Mais bien sûr.* Of course, Monsieur. Babette, bring Monsieur an Armagnac."

An hour before midnight, Hunkeler was sitting in his kitchen with a half-empty pot of tea in front of him. Next to it sat the two cats, busily cleaning themselves. Every now and then they paused and gave Hunkeler a surprised look, as if they hadn't expected him to be here. Then they would resume their cleaning and purring. They weren't supposed to be on the table, they knew that perfectly well. But tonight Hunkeler was just glad to have two friendly creatures near him.

The temperature outside had dropped sharply, it was at least fifteen degrees below freezing. He had felt the cold on his short drive home from Knoeringue, the engine had barely warmed up. There were so many stars in the sky, more than he thought he'd ever seen before. When he got out of the car in front of his house, he'd stood and stared in awe. It was a sea of lights up there, deep and bright, with Orion spread across at a tilt. The nut tree was covered in hoar frost, like heavenly tinsel on a magical plant of the night.

He'd gone in and placed more wood on the dying embers, then switched on the electric night heating. He would have liked to drive to Colmar, but he had things to do the following day.

He called Hedwig.

She was still chipper. "What's up, old man?"

"It's another magical night," he said. "I've never seen so many stars."

"I see you're in a poetic mood. Carry on, I'm happy to listen."

"I'm not. I've heard a terrible story. They hung up a group of young men, here in the area, during the last war."

"Is that why you've called me?"

"I need to talk to someone. Don't you understand that? You're the only one I have."

She giggled now, she liked hearing that.

"Say something," he begged her. "I want to hear your voice."

She thought for a while, then she realized. "On meathooks?"

"Yes, it seems that's what happened. I'm not sure though."

"So, you're up to your eyeballs in another case. Why don't you leave it with your colleagues and come and join us here?"

"Because I'm in too deep," he shouted. "Is that so hard to grasp? I can't walk away from it now." Then, a little more quietly: "Sorry. I know I shouldn't shout. But it's so frustrating it makes me want to howl."

"Hunkeler, the lone wolf, howling into the polar night. Do you think anyone can hear you?"

"Yes, you."

"Right. Now sort yourself out," she commanded. "You do what you need to do. Who knows, perhaps you'll succeed again. That's what you want, isn't it? To succeed?"

He made an effort not to start shouting again. "I just want to know what, how and why it happened. That's all."

"There's a young man hanging here too, in the Unterlinden Museum. Jesus of Nazareth, painted by Grünewald. Four reports were written on the what, how and why of his murder, the four Gospels. They don't change the fact that a dead man is hanging on the Cross. I looked at him for an hour this morning. I'm asking myself why. Do you follow me?"

"Keep talking," he pleaded.

"The image is almost unbearable. I wonder how Grünewald managed it five hundred years ago. It felt like I had watched a man die on the Cross. And now there was a corpse hanging there. And I was still watching. The crazy thing is, as terrible as the image is, it's also sublime and you don't want to take your eyes off it. Why is that? Do you know? I'm going to go back there tomorrow. Why do we gaze at death with such fascination?"

"Yesterday evening I talked to a guy who said that death is the only firm reality. Perhaps that's why."

"OK, I'll think of that tomorrow," she said. "Sleep tight. And don't howl too loudly."

"Wait," he said. "I'm coming to Colmar at the weekend. Will you still be there?"

"If you're coming, sure. But come on Saturday. So we can have a nice night together."

He lifted the pot off the tea warmer, refilled his mug and drank slowly. The tea tasted bitter, it had been left to steep for too long. He loved the bitterness, it was good for his bowels and his thoughts.

The cats interrupted their cleaning regime and watched him. When he didn't shoo them away, they got back to licking their paws.

He called Lüdi.

"*Oui, mon joujou?*"

"It's Hunkeler. Have you got a moment?"

"Not really," Lüdi replied. "I'm expecting a call from my boyfriend any minute. Keep it short."

"How did the briefing go?"

"Oh yes." There it was, the chuckle, almost silent. "Bardet has found something. A grave on B35. Not under the cabin, they dug there in vain."

"What do you mean, a grave?"

"A grave made of concrete, close to the yew tree. It contained Flückiger's past."

"Well come on then, fire away!" Hunkeler barked, causing the cats to leap from the table in alarm.

"There was a photo of a young woman who could be Sonja Flückiger. It actually resembles the picture in today's tabloid."

"What else?"

"There was an old gun from the Wehrmacht. And the collar of a uniform with two tabs. The collar tab on the right shows the SS insignia. On the left tab is the corporal insignia. That means Russius was a corporal in the SS. So, the OF on the postcard from Altkirch could stand for Obersturmführer. Are you still there?"

"No, I'm somewhere completely different. I'm sitting in an Emmental kitchen, drinking chicory coffee."

"Have you gone nuts?"

Hunkeler didn't reply.

"It gets even better," Lüdi continued. "The grave also contained an Iron Cross 2nd Class, complete with certificate, issued by a General Lammerding. He was the commandant of the SS division Das Reich. According to Bardet, that division was responsible for the Oradour massacre on 10 June 1944."

"Why don't they know about this in Potsdam?"

"Because former SS people aren't keen on popping up in the military history research office. At least that's what they told us."

"Why didn't Russius throw the stuff away?"

"As I've already said, Russius was possibly a very lonely, itinerant person, who had a constant need to surround himself with friends. Perhaps the SS had been his home. You don't just throw away your home. Also, they've re-examined the corpse, in particular the tattoo under the left upper arm, the rose. Apparently that's where SS members had their blood group tattooed in. And guess what?"

Yes, Hunkeler could guess.

"Under Russius's left arm, if you look closely, you can still see the blood group, covered by the rose," Lüdi informed him.

"Hang on, I need a piss," said Hunkeler. "Don't hang up." He went out the front and waded through the deep snow to the nut tree. He peed against the trunk, his eyes cast upwards at the frosted branches that glimmered in the light from the hallway. He drew the ice-cold air deep into his lungs. The clinking of a chain could be heard from the cowshed across the yard. When he'd mulled things over, he went back into the kitchen. "Are you still there?" he asked.

"Yes, but I'd prefer not to be. What if he rings and the line is busy?"

"He'll just have to wait, your *joujou*. Listen. In February 1943 a group of young men were arrested in this area after they tried to escape to Switzerland. A neighbour told me that those lads were shot and hung up with meathooks. Apparently by the SS."

"No, that's unbelievable!"

"I'm driving to Ballersdorf tomorrow to see what I can find out. I'll fill everyone in at the afternoon briefing. Sleep tight, my darling."

He picked up the two cats, carried them into Hedwig's room and set them down on the bed. Then he undressed, opened the window onto the garden and crawled under the red and white checked covers. He listened to the cats purring, and after a while he heard two owls calling from afar.

The following morning around nine Hunkeler was driving along the Altkirch bypass. It was Friday, 6 January. The area here was undergoing rapid change, with car repair shops, warehouses and shopping centres springing up. There were trucks travelling along the icy road, and a tractor with a trailer stacked high with enormous hay bales. Up on the left was Altkirch's old town. He turned onto the Route Nationale up to Ballersdorf, which was lined by bare trees. When he reached the top, he could see the Belfort Gap and the blue Vosges mountains to the right.

Ballersdorf cemetery was at the entrance to the village, on the left. From there the road gently dipped back down to the church. There were plenty of parking spaces. Hunkeler placed his firearm into the glove compartment and got out.

EN MÉMOIRE DES FUSILLÉS DU 13 ET DU 17 FÉVRIER 1943 was written on the wall in front of the church. In memory of those executed by firing squad on 13 and 17 February 1943. Below stood seventeen names, four with the surname Wiest. Wiest, wasn't that also the name of the girlfriend of Moritz Hänggi who rented B26? But this didn't seem relevant any more.

He stayed standing in front of the wall for a while. An old woman climbed the snow-covered steps to the church, presumably going in to pray. A tanker with a trailer came driving down the road from the direction of the cemetery. Its engine revved as it disappeared around the bend to Belfort.

Hunkeler carried on walking towards the village. To the left was a brasserie advertising *carpes frites, Kangourou* and *Surlawerla,* baked carp, kangaroo meat and liver in soured cream sauce. To the right was the municipal building.

He entered and found himself in a small, well-heated room that contained a table and a desk. The desk was covered in stacks of paper. Behind the table sat a woman who was talking to a young couple. There was a chair by the wall, and Hunkeler sat down and waited.

He listened to their conversation. They were speaking fast and in French. The couple wanted to get married, that much he understood. Not in the church, just in the registry office, but they wanted a proper ceremony. They were asking how best to arrange this. Would there be glasses available for champagne, was there a coffee machine? Where would the flowers go? Was the parish responsible for organizing a photographer? Was it permitted to throw rice grains over the newlyweds? The woman behind the table answered all their questions with the patience of a saint.

After twenty minutes, the couple left, clearly satisfied.

"*Et vous? Qu'est-ce que vous voulez?* How can I help?" the woman asked Hunkeler.

As always in administrative settings like these, he began to stutter. He tried to summon his best French, then gave up. "Do you speak Alsatian?" he asked.

"*Non, je regrette.*"

"Is the mayor in?"

"*Oui, un moment.*"

She disappeared through a door. He waited ten minutes. He didn't light up, smoking was not permitted. The snow on his shoes had long melted away. The room was overheated, he took off his jacket.

Finally, a man in his fifties with a guarded expression and intelligent eyes appeared. He asked what Hunkeler wanted.

Hunkeler said that he was from Basel and a writer. That he was currently writing a crime novel which took place in this area. Was there a book about the history of Ballersdorf?

The man nodded, took a book from a shelf and handed it to Hunkeler. He leafed through it. It was in German and had been published in 1929.

"That doesn't help me," Hunkeler said. "I need something about February 1943, about the seventeen young men who were executed."

"Why?"

"As you may have heard, a man was found hanging from a meathook on the border to Basel in the early hours of New Year's Day. My novel is based on that. There's a trail that leads to Ballersdorf 1943."

The man was unmoved, he didn't believe a single word. "Someone from the Police Nationale has been here," he said. "He also asked about February 1943. But he didn't claim to be writing a novel."

"What was his name?"

"I've forgotten. If you're a Basel cop, you have no business being here. You know that."

Hunkeler felt like strangling him. But he stayed calm. "I'm looking for an Anton Russius, he was a member of the SS. Does anybody in Ballersdorf know that name?"

"No."

"But they shot seventeen young men here in Ballersdorf in February 1943. Or isn't that true?"

"No. In Struthof."

"And about them being hung up with meathooks, do you know anything about that?"

"No. Please excuse me, I have work to do. I'd appreciate it if you could leave the room now." He smiled briefly, the meeting was over. "You know, we Alsatians believe the dead should be left to rest."

Hunkeler walked back up the road towards the cemetery. He was boiling with anger. He really was a complete idiot, the trick with the crime writer had utterly failed. Evidently he had the kind of face that signalled "police officer" a mile off.

The stubborn bastard at the municipal office, Hunkeler thought, why would the man not come out with the truth? What was he hiding? Then he remembered Beat Jau in Rüegsbach. He'd been just as reticent. These village chieftains couldn't bear people sticking their noses in. Hunkeler could understand that. He didn't like it either.

He pushed open the iron gate to the cemetery. The graves were lined up in neat rows. Many of them had recently been visited, the snow on the side paths had been tamped down. A large cross stood against the back wall. À LA MÉMOIRE DE NOS ENFANTS FUSILLÉS AU CAMP DE STRUTHOF, it read: in memory of our children, who were executed at the Struthof camp. Ten names were listed below, the names of the lads from Ballersdorf. The snow in front of the cross was untouched, nobody had set foot in it.

Hunkeler waded through the deep snow, feeling helpless and excluded. What was he doing here? This wretched story was none of his business.

He looked at the twenty-four war graves. MORT POUR LA FRANCE, died for France, in the First and the Second World War. Among them was also a COMBATTANT FRANÇAIS INCONNU, an unknown French soldier who had remained nameless.

He glanced over the wall at a gently rising hill where a farm stood. He saw the two silo towers and recognized the smell of maize silage. Then he realized there was someone behind him. He turned round.

It was an old man. He was unshaven and the collar of a white nightgown could be seen poking above the neckline of his jacket.

"*Sueche Sie eppis?* Are you looking for something, Monsieur?"

"No, not really," Hunkeler replied. "You made me jump. You came so quietly, I didn't hear you."

"I'm sorry. I was visiting my Marie, she's buried over there." He pointed to a grave at the front. "I saw you come in. I followed you, and now I'm here. Are you from Basel?"

"What makes you think that?"

"Because there's a car with a Basel plate parked in front of the church. The people of Basel are lucky. They have no war graves. Over there, those eight graves are from November 1944. I was eight then. The SS was up there." He pointed at the hill next to the farm. "They had the new Tiger tanks. They were undefeatable. But then they ran out of fuel, so they couldn't move any more. We boys watched as the French gunned down one after the other." He tried to chuckle, but it was difficult. He'd left his false teeth at home. "I live over there." He indicated a small red brick house on the edge of the village. "It's not far to the cemetery for me. But first I always go to the brasserie. That's why I saw your car."

"The ten lads from Ballersdorf whose names are listed here, are they buried here?" Hunkeler asked.

"No. Nobody knows where they're buried. Their bodies and the bodies of the others who didn't come from Ballersdorf were taken to the crematorium in Strasbourg. That's all I know. That's all anybody knows. Why are you interested in them?"

"I have a house here in the area. My neighbour, an old farmer, was also conscripted. He was taken to Karlsruhe. He ran away and was lucky. They hid him at home."

"Yes, many wanted to run away back then. Stalingrad fell at the end of January. We knew then that the Germans had lost the war. Of course, we all listened to Radio Sottens. I don't personally remember that though. My mother told me."

"What can you personally remember?" Hunkeler asked.

"The following morning was a Sunday, I can remember that. Three of them had been shot dead at the railway embankment that night, by a German patrol. One got away. The others ran home. On Sunday morning they came to early Mass with their parents as if nothing had happened. The Gestapo fetched them out and took them to Struthof. I can remember that very clearly, how they were hauled out of Mass. The whole village prayed. It didn't help."

"Where had the Gestapo come from?"

"I don't know. Suddenly there were SS and Gestapo men everywhere. We had to stay in our houses for several days, with the shutters closed. The SS wanted to burn down the whole village. Our mayor ran to the headquarters in Altkirch and begged for mercy. That helped. In any case, our village is still standing." Again he tried to chuckle. He was standing in the snow in his red boots as if rooted to the spot.

"I heard that their bodies were hung up with meathooks," Hunkeler ventured.

"I've heard that too. That's what they say, *n'est-ce pas*? But it isn't true. Who would do such a thing? People made that up, to express their anger."

"Did you know a Russius?"

"A what? A Russian?"

Hunkeler hesitated, then he nodded.

"There was a Russian with the SS, that's true. A corporal. He was the worst of them all, everybody knew him. He came to the early Mass too, with a machine gun."

"Do you know what became of this Russian?"

"No, I don't know that. He left, together with the other SS people. No idea where they went. You know, Monsieur, we don't like to talk about those times. *C'est passé*. Come, my feet are getting cold."

Together they tramped through the snow towards the exit.

"Why did you tell me all those things?" Hunkeler asked.

"Perhaps because I was visiting Marie's grave when you came into the cemetery. And because you were standing there, all alone in front of the war graves."

Hunkeler drove back to Altkirch. He turned off towards the old town centre and parked. What he needed now was a touch of normality, some joie de vivre, a pinch of cheeriness. He walked along the Rue Charles de Gaulle and looked at the window display of a butcher's shop, where a huge number of sausages were laid out. Next to it was a bakery with red, yellow and green confectionery. A basket full of baguettes stood at the back, and arranged on a shelf beside it were the loaves containing olives, sesame and sunflower seeds so favoured these days. Further along was a shop selling winter sports equipment. They had jackets in bright yellow, brilliant white and intense blue, insulated with down, for temperatures as low as minus forty degrees. Skis for classic cross-country, for freestyle, for touring and for downhill. Single and two-seater toboggans.

He noticed that people seemed to enjoy walking along this street. Only rarely did anyone come along by themselves, people were mostly in twos and threes. He wondered whether they had all come out of their apartments alone and had bumped into someone, then joined them for a chat.

"Where are you off to? The butchers? I might as well tag along."

He felt pretty stupid here on this street. He noticed people looking at him curiously. He walked a little faster, as though he was headed somewhere in particular. He came to the town hall, which was bathed in sunshine. He recognized it, then he remembered he'd seen it on one of the postcards.

He turned round and went into a bookshop. A girl, presumably a trainee, asked whether he was looking for something.

Did they have anything on Ballersdorf 1943, he enquired.

"What is Ballersdorf 1943?"

"Ballersdorf, *mille neuf cent quarante-trois*," he clarified. "*Le massacre.*"

"*Ah, oui.*" She remembered and led him to the local history shelf. "*Voilà.*" She pulled out a book entitled *Et si c'était moi!* He leafed through it. It was an Alsatian family memoir spanning several generations. Plenty of French pathos, very few facts. He only bought it out of courtesy.

As he stood at the till to pay, an old woman addressed him. He knew her, but she had to remind him of her name. It was Margot. She and her husband Charles ran a small shop in Jettingen, where you could buy tinned food, wine and men's belts. Hunkeler knew Charles had been imprisoned in Russia, in Tambov, where he'd lost his toes to frostbite. He also knew that, having been captured as a German soldier, Charles received a lifelong annuity from Germany, which his neighbours envied him for.

"How is your husband?" Hunkeler asked.

"Not well," she replied. "He can't bear the cold. He's in hospital, here in Altkirch. I have to bring him crossword puzzles so he can while away the hours. German ones, he doesn't understand the French puzzles. I ordered six German crossword magazines, but they're not here."

"*Non,*" the girl said. "*Je regrette. Venez demain.*"

"I come every morning," Margot replied. "But the magazines are never here."

The girl shrugged her shoulders, rather flippantly, Hunkeler thought. "Give my regards to Charles," he said, and left.

He drove through the villages. Wittersdorf, Tagsdorf, Hundsbach, Franken. Old half-timbered houses, some of them quite dilapidated, others renovated in all manner of colours. They were surrounded by the red-brick homes of cross-border commuters. It was a kind of no man's land outside the gates of Basel, hidden and inconspicuous. Every victorious army had marched through here, leaving scorched earth behind.

He parked in front of the inn at Jettingen. It too was an old, half-timbered house. *Nibble, nibble, gnaw, who is nibbling at my little house?* A few logs smouldered in the fireplace the landlord had installed in the middle of the room. Unemployed men sat at the bar with their glasses of wine. They took a close interest in what Hunkeler was ordering. He asked for a small coffee.

Somewhat sullenly, he skimmed through the book he had bought. He'd hoped to get something more factual, a historical account, with a bit less of the personal touch. Still, he found what he was looking for.

On the night of 7 February 1943, eighteen young men from Riespach and its surroundings had set off towards the Swiss border. The Swiss authorities sent them back to the Belfort area.

On the night of 10 February 1943, 183 men left for Switzerland. They took two German border guards hostage. Once they had crossed the border they set them free again. This group was known as the Espen convoy, as the men had gathered in a place called Espen.

On the night of 12 February 1943, another eighteen men set out to reach Switzerland, this time from the Ballersdorf area. They ran into the hands of a German patrol. Three of the lads and a German infantryman were fatally shot. The following morning, fourteen of the young men were arrested, taken to Struthof and shot. One managed to escape to Switzerland.

There was no mention of meathooks in the book.

Hunkeler wondered why it was so difficult to get at the facts. Didn't the people of Altkirch want to know what happened in their region sixty years ago? Perhaps they really did believe the dead should be left to rest. But that didn't work. It never worked.

Shortly before twelve, Hunkeler entered the inn at Knoeringue and sat down at the Scholler family table. Preparations for lunch were in full swing. Babette was placing jugs of water and wine on the tables, old Frau Scholler was bringing out soup bowls. There was meat broth with marrowbone, boiled beef for main course and a pudding of preserved plums. He didn't want anything yet, he was waiting for Monsieur Rinser.

He heard the church bells strike twelve. Shortly after, the room filled up within a matter of minutes. Only one table in the back corner on the right remained free. The customers were mainly tradespeople, who walked in and ladled soup into their bowls as if they lived here. They were all in their work clothes. Plasterers in white outfits, electricians with pliers in their pockets, carpenters, bricklayers. Also delivery drivers for breweries like Kronenbourg and Mützig Pils. Nobody said much, the men were tired and wanted to rest. The radio was tuned to Südwestrundfunk 4, the usual selection of German hits.

At half past, an old, slightly stooping man came in, accompanied by a young, pale fellow. They sat down at the free table. Frau Scholler went over, talked to them, then waved at Hunkeler to come and join them.

Old Konrad Rinser was a stately and striking-looking man. Astute, with an open gaze and clear pronunciation, he spoke slowly and precisely. The young man was rather odd, Hunkeler couldn't figure him out. His hands were permanently shaking and he seemed to be looking everywhere and nowhere. He ate very little. As soon as he'd laid down his spoon, he lit a cigarette.

"Frau Scholler told me about you," Hunkeler said. "She says you can remember what happened in February 1943."

"That's right," said Rinser. "I was in the Espen convoy. Why do you want to know about it? Frau Scholler says you're a police officer from Basel."

"I'm cooperating on a murder case. Under the direction of the Police Nationale." Hunkeler smiled warmly, trying to reel out his old charm.

"I heard about that," Rinser commented. "But this murder can't possibly have anything to do with Ballersdorf. That story about the meathooks isn't true. They were shot in Struthof and transported to Strasbourg in wooden crates, two in each crate."

"So how did that story come about? Who invented it?"

"I don't know. People should have told the truth, clear and simple, *n'est-ce pas?*"

"You're wrong," the young man protested. "It wasn't invented."

"And how would you know about that?" Rinser asked him.

"Because I know," he replied.

"This is my great-nephew, Claude Schwob," said Rinser. "He's my sister's grandson. She married a Schwob."

"Pleased to meet you," said Hunkeler. "So, where do you live, what work do you do?"

"*Pourquoi?* You have no right to ask me. We're not in Switzerland here."

"He works for the Crédit Mutuel in Jettingen," Rinser replied. "He's a computer specialist. Every night he sits in front of his screen until past one. What the devil he does there, I don't know. He lives in a farmhouse in Franken. I've told him he should get some hens. Then he'd have to get up early in the morning. But he doesn't want to."

"*Tais-toi,*" Claude hissed, barely audible.

Hunkeler placed a nice piece of meat on his plate. He helped himself to dumplings, cranberries and half a pear. Then he topped up his wine and drank. "So, in your opinion it's true," he said.

"No. In my opinion you don't have the right to ask me."

Hunkeler popped a piece of meat into his mouth. It was juicy and tender. He went to put down his knife, but it fell on the floor. He quickly bent down to pick it up. Yes, the young man was wearing sports shoes.

"What the hell are you doing?" Claude hissed. "What kind of Stone Age method is that? Anyway, what do you want from me, Monsieur?"

Hunkeler acted surprised. "From you? I don't want anything from you. You can't possibly know. You weren't even born at the time."

Claude's face went white. He nearly threw down his knife and fork, but he kept his temper in check and shoved a piece of dumpling into his mouth with a shaky hand.

"*Mais Claude*, what's the matter?" Rinser asked him.

"*Rien*," he replied. "Nothing."

"So, what do you want to know?" Rinser asked.

"I'd like to know what you did back then, in early February 1943."

"I got the conscription notice. But I knew I didn't want to go to Russia."

"But it was dangerous, trying to escape to Switzerland. You didn't even know whether you'd get across the border."

"The Eastern Front would have been even more dangerous. If I was going to bite the dust, then I might as well do it here in Alsace. That's what we all thought. We had nothing against the Russians. We were glad when we heard Stalingrad was surrounded. And to be carted off to the Eastern Front as cannon fodder, *non merci*."

Claude shoved a couple of plums into his mouth and got up. He was even thinner than he had seemed when he'd been sitting down. "*Au revoir*," he said, and left.

"He's always telling me how we should have fought against the Wehrmacht," commented Rinser. "Even though it was impossible."

Hunkeler had a couple more of the plums. They were wonderfully sweet, served with a shot of plum brandy.

"Were the German border guards not keeping a lookout when you went across?"

"No. They only kept proper watch two days later, on the twelfth. We came across a couple of infantrymen. But there were so many of us, there wasn't anything they could do. We took two of them with us as hostages. That's to say, I didn't even notice any of that. I simply followed everyone else."

"Where did you cross?"

"From Seppois, towards Bonfol. There was a big inn just over the border. We waited there until morning. They were good people, they gave us food and drink. Two girls brought it to us. None of us could sleep, of course. We didn't know whether we'd be sent back."

"And then where did you end up?"

"We were loaded onto trucks under strict watch and taken to a prison in Pruntrut. The following night, we slept in hallways and on stairs. Then we got the news that we could stay." Rinser hadn't eaten much of the meat, but he spooned up all the plums. "Everyone whooped with joy. I joined in too, even though I was married. I had a wife and a newborn at home. Later I learned in a roundabout way that my wife had to go to Germany, somewhere near Ulm. As a forced labourer."

"And the newborn?"

"It stayed with an aunt." He chewed the plums slowly. He was completely absorbed in recalling everything. But it took strength. "We were taken to a camp in Büren on the Aare river, near Biel. It was terrible. We thought that once we were in free Switzerland, we'd be able to move around freely. That wasn't the case at all. Barbed wire and guards and shouting all day long. We weren't allowed to go out to have a beer. We were kept like prisoners."

Hunkeler didn't say anything. He knew that was how it had been.

"After four months, I was assigned to a farmer in the Zurich Oberland. I was very happy that I could finally work. But it was hell. He kept me like a second-class citizen. I had to work from early morning to late at night. Sundays too. And he barely paid me anything. So I went to the police station and asked to be taken back to Büren. And that's what happened, although it wasn't Büren, they took me to a camp in Valais. I can't remember what it was called. But if I try hard, it might come back to me." He smiled amiably and loosened his collar, which was held together by a tie. The collar button was missing.

"No need," Hunkeler told him. "Please carry on. Would you like some coffee?"

"Yes please."

Hunkeler ordered coffee from Babette.

"Eventually I ended up on another farm, in the Bernese Seeland. The people there were friendly, they were kind to me. I stayed there until Alsace was liberated. Then I returned home straight away, to be with my child. My wife came home after me, as Ulm was liberated later. We visited the people in Seeland several times over the years, with the whole family. And they've also come to stay with us."

They both sipped the bittersweet coffee.

"How about a brandy?" Hunkeler asked.

"Why not."

The inn had emptied, and Babette started clearing the tables.

"Were you able to keep in touch with your family?"

"Yes. Every now and then, new people would arrive. We helped each other out as best we could. One time, the lad who had managed to escape on the twelfth of February turned up. He told us about Ballersdorf. It was a shock for us all."

"Did you know someone called Anton Russius? He was an SS man stationed in Ballersdorf."

Rinser thought for a long time. "I'm terrible with names, you see. Much of it I can remember very clearly. The mess tins in the camp. The pea and barley soup. But the names have all gone." He thought a while longer. "If I'm not mistaken, I've heard people speak of a Russian who was in Ballersdorf. He must have been a truly horrible person. Why do you ask?"

"Is there a reason I shouldn't?"

"Claude has already asked me about him. Several times in fact. What was his name again?"

"Anton Russius."

"That's right. Claude asked me about someone called Anton Russius. I told him the same as I've told you."

"That's odd," remarked Hunkeler. "I mean, where did your great-nephew get that name from?"

"He takes an interest in that period. He spends half the night surfing on his computer. That's what they call it, *n'est- ce pas?*"

Hunkeler nodded.

"I almost think he may be a hacker," Rinser continued. "I know he was summoned to Mulhouse one time. But they didn't have any evidence against him. He also has friends who share his views. I wouldn't be surprised if they intend to liberate Alsace once and for all." He chuckled so much about his joke, he was shaking with laughter. Then he looked around to check whether anyone had spotted him. But Hunkeler was the only one who'd laughed along. "That was a bad joke, I know," said Rinser. "We're part of France for good now. *S'isch i Ornig so.* It's OK." He closed his eyes as he drained his brandy glass. "A few years ago, we all met up again," he told Hunkeler. "Well, only those who were still alive of course. We met at that inn across the border. It's no longer open to the public, but the house is still standing. There were quite a few of us. Two old women also came along. They were the two girls who had brought the food and drink out to us back then. We all hugged each other and kissed. We cried and sang songs."

Hunkeler slowly drove back to Basel. The giant maize silo outside Muespach-le-Haut looked solemn in the winter light. On the left was the Restaurant Zur Ausweiche, where trains travelling on the old single-track line had used a siding to avoid each other. He passed the Täufer farm, where the cows were standing outside despite the cold. Beyond the pale water tower of Folgensbourg he glimpsed a broad expanse of snow-covered fields. Down on the plain, the airport lights were already on.

Three Police Nationale cars were parked outside the French custom house. The Swiss customs post was unmanned. Hunkeler could hear the clattering of the conveyor belt over at the gravel quarry, they were working in the tower. Rinaldi's hole in the fence had been repaired. Hunkeler slowed down to a walking pace and took a close look. Yes, someone had used a fair amount of barbed wire there. That's what happened, thought Hunkeler, either side of the border. If someone didn't know what to do, they simply resorted to barbed wire, without any regard for injuries.

Haller was standing at the allotment entrance with his Alsatian colleague, puffing a trail of smoke into the air.

"Any news?" Hunkeler asked.

"Madörin is nuts," Haller told him. "He's gone and arrested Stebler, and Rinaldi too. Just because they crawled through the fence."

"How did he know?"

"Apparently he saw their tracks."

"How? He's not even allowed into the allotments."

"He saw the hole in the fence and crawled through. Though he claims not to have set foot in France. He says the fence is exactly on the border."

"What an idiot. Who is he chasing anyway?"

"He swears it was one of the allotment holders."

"And Cattaneo?"

"What about Cattaneo?" Haller asked.

"Didn't he take Cattaneo into custody?"

"Not as far as I know. Do you know anything about that?" Haller asked his colleague.

"*Non*," his colleague replied. "*Mais je m'en fous.* I couldn't care less."

*

Hunkeler went into the Blume. Siegrist and Schläpfer were sitting at the regulars' table. Cattaneo was there too, lost in thought. The landlady stood behind the bar. There was no one else in the room.

"Good afternoon," Hunkeler greeted them cheerily. "How is everyone? May I?" He sat down next to the men and reached for the tabloid lying on the table. "A cup of coffee please, with cold milk."

Nobody said a word, nobody moved. Hunkeler didn't care. He read up on what the eager fellows in Zurich had found out.

An article entitled "What's behind the rose?" revealed that the mysterious Russian from Rüegsbach had a rose tattoo under his left upper arm. This had been gleaned from one of his secret lovers. Question: *Who would choose to have a rose tattooed under their left upper arm?* Answer: *Nobody, unless they had a good reason. What reason could that be? Because he wanted to hide something. And what did he want to hide?*

The tabloid could further reveal that according to well-informed historical circles, young men entering the SS used to have their blood group inked in under their left upper arm. It was a symbolic mark that bound them to the Schutzstaffel for life.

Question: *Did the mysterious Russian Flückiger serve in the SS?* Answer: *Quite possibly. The key to this question was hidden under the rose tattoo.*

Further question: *What are the Basel authorities trying to hide? Is Basel CID shielding a war criminal?*

So they hadn't found out the name. The collection for the destitute Sonja with the three paper roses had reached nearly 160,000 francs so far. The paper was appealing for further donations.

Hunkeler marvelled, despite his anger. They were pretty quick off the mark, those fellows. It was just a question of time before they found the trail that led to Alsace.

He briefly looked around. Still nobody had said a word. And there was no cup of coffee on the table either. He picked up the *Basler Zeitung* and leafed through it. He found a photo of Bardet standing in front of Ferati's burned-down cabin. The report beside it stated that the Basel police had detained several allotment holders for questioning, including some foreign nationals.

"Is there no coffee today?" he asked.

"No," the landlady replied. "The machine is broken."

"What do you think of this report about the rose tattoo?" Hunkeler asked.

Silence all round.

"I didn't put Stebler behind bars," he said. "And not the others either. That was Officer Madörin's work."

"It wasn't any of us allotment holders," Siegrist finally said. "I'd stake my life on that. Nor do we believe that Flückiger was in the SS."

"Well, we need to get to the truth as quickly as possible," said Hunkeler. "Otherwise the tabloid people will. And they'll really milk it."

"We don't care," Siegrist replied. "It's a Zurich paper."

"Did anyone know about the tattoo?"

"Why would we? We don't go looking under each other's arms."

Hunkeler waited a while. He didn't know how else to break the silence.

"We're destined to die," muttered Cattaneo without looking up from his schnapps. "Nothing is born that does not have an end. The end lies in the beginning. Everything that has a beginning and an end passes. Only death persists."

"Stop it, will you," Schläpfer groaned. "You're driving me crazy."

"He's always coming out with this kind of stuff," commented Siegrist. "There's no helping him."

"How long has he been talking like that?" Hunkeler asked.

"It must be four years now. Sometimes he's completely normal. Then he falls back into the philosophizing. And now Giovanna has gone and left him."

"It's him you should arrest," said Schläpfer. "Not Stebler and the others. He could do with someone keeping an eye on him."

Hunkeler hesitated. Then he fished out his notebook, tore out a page and wrote his phone number on it. He put the note on the table in front of Cattaneo. "This is my number. Please call me if you need to talk, man to man."

"Why man to man?" Cattaneo asked. "Why not man to woman?"

"Now can I finally get that coffee, for God's sake?" Hunkeler asked.

"No," the landlady replied from behind the bar. "The machine is still broken."

There wasn't much time before the briefing, which had been set for 5 p.m. But there was something else he wanted to know.

He parked in front of the Luzernerring and went in. He ordered an espresso and lit a cigarette to distract himself. It didn't work, he didn't feel like pulling the smoke down into his lungs. Later, he thought, and stubbed it out. Later, when everything was resolved. Then he would smoke a cigarette with relish.

Mara brought him the espresso. She stayed by the table and adjusted her hair. "And?" she asked.

He stirred sugar into the cup and drank. A gulp of life, a few bitter drops.

"Have you got any leads?"

"How about the rose you didn't tell me about?" he asked her.

"It had almost completely faded away, you could barely see it."

"Did you know what he was hiding underneath?"

"I didn't know, but I had a hunch," she said. "Where I come from, people are aware of these things."

"And you just left me running in circles?"

"Must you know everything? Doesn't everyone have their secrets?"

"But you were happy enough to tell the tabloid. Did they pay you well at least?"

The colour drained from her face. "Are you crazy? Why are you insulting me?"

She went back to the bar. When he left, she didn't look at him.

Prosecutor Suter opened the briefing. He was dressed in a pale flannel suit with a sky-blue tie and seemed to be the only one still feeling chipper. Sadly, he had an important appointment to go to, he said right at the start. He would have to leave shortly. The investigation was approaching a critical point, he informed them. It was time to crack it, by hook or by crook. He could sense this, he said, thanks to his extensive experience. The cooperation with the Police Nationale was now well established, which meant his presence was no longer essential.

He beamed at Madame Godet, who smiled sweetly back at him in return. Unfortunately, Suter continued, Commissaire Bardet was unable to attend at this time, as he was out investigating. If possible, he would join them before the meeting was over. Then he looked around victoriously. "We have managed to gain a significant and unassailable edge on certain sectors of the media. We have left the hacks well behind. So, for now we have upheld the primacy of government-run investigative bodies. This is a great success, for which I would like to congratulate you all. Thank you, Madame, thank you, Messieurs." He gave a hint of a bow and left the room. A powerful exit indeed.

An awkward silence now settled over the room. Madame Godet sat bolt upright in her chair, with the backrest jutting out above her head. Lüdi giggled helplessly. He looked exhausted and had dark rings under his eyes. Madörin nervously drummed his fingers on the tabletop. It was clear this briefing was turning into a farce.

"Why was Russius's body not examined more closely at the start?" Hunkeler asked. "It would have saved us a lot of bother."

Madame Godet smiled cheerily. "Because it didn't occur to anyone that there was much to be discovered, Monsieur."

"There's a woman from the Balkans who works at the Luzernerring," Hunkeler continued. "She knew about it."

"So why didn't she tell you? Are your charms no longer sufficient to sweet-talk a waitress?"

Hunkeler didn't reply. The tension was getting close to unbearable. A tension which arose from uncertainty. "Is there any further information from Potsdam?" he asked.

"No," Lüdi replied, "nothing new."

"*Mais oui, Messieurs*," said Madame Godet. "We have the Iron Cross and the collar tabs. We must work with what we have."

"What else was found in the ground under the yew tree?" Lüdi asked her.

"Not much. Everything is being closely examined."

"I can't stand this nonsense any more," declared Madörin. "Iron Cross and rose tattoo, it's all humbug."

"Humbug," enquired Madame Godet, "what is that?"

"Rubbish, nonsense. It might be great pulp fiction fodder for a sentimental story in the tabloids. But it's no use for detective work on the ground. How are the three roses relevant to Flückiger's murder? What's the old bird in Rüegsbach got to do with the meathook Flückiger was hanging from? OK, now they're collecting money for her. But we in this room have the task of finding out who killed Anton Flückiger."

Nobody spoke. Everyone was agreed on that.

"Pfister and Dogan, and now Stebler and Rinaldi too," said Lüdi. "We can't put all the allotment holders behind bars. And most importantly, we can't keep them here indefinitely. The magistrate won't allow it."

"Yes, we can," Madörin countered. "We can if we want to.

And I absolutely want to. I've known people like that since childhood, I grew up in those circles. I know the fervent hatred they're capable of. They would floor a complete stranger over a dented bumper. When it comes to a dead rabbit, they'd easily exterminate an entire family. And Flückiger was just that type of guy. What was he, what did he have, after all? He had nothing, he worked in a warehouse. What does that mean, gentlemen?" He struck a pose, as if he was a lawyer delivering a final speech. "It means slaving away from seven in the morning to six in the evening. Not in a heated office but in a draughty depot. For little pay. It also means continuously being ticked off by the boss. A man like him has to stomach a lot in his working life. There comes a time when he spews it all out again, in the form of brutal aggression. The only thing that astonishes me is that he buried his army pistol. I wouldn't be surprised if he got himself a newer gun at some point."

"That's entirely possible," Madame Godet agreed. "We found a wax cloth under one of the floorboards. It's probable that the oil stains on the cloth are from gun oil."

"And you wait until now to tell us that?" Madörin bellowed.

"*Oui, Monsieur.* I was under no obligation to tell you. And please stop shouting at me. Otherwise I will leave the room."

"Apologies, Madame," Madörin replied. He tried to smile, but failed thoroughly. Like a terrier trying not to bare its teeth. "I think Flückiger was shot with his own weapon. I think it was him who smashed up Ferati's barbecue and killed Füglistaller's rabbits. And I think he broke into Begovič and Dogan's cabins. I think he spread hate and terror among his peers. For the simple reason that he despised himself. And in the early hours of New Year's Day, one of those men got back at him, with his own gun."

"But how?" asked Madame Godet. "The gun was hidden under the floorboards."

"I think Flückiger sensed he was in danger and got the gun out to protect himself. It must have been lying on the table when the killer came in."

"*C'est possible.* We also found oil stains on the table."

"Why not Cattaneo?" Hunkeler asked. "If I remember correctly, they also found his prints in the cabin."

Madörin shook his head. "No, not Cattaneo. He's too riven by grief. He wouldn't have been able to muster enough hate for the deed."

"And what's happening about Cannibal Frost?" Lüdi asked. "Did you check up on them?"

Madörin looked at them, a little uncertain. Everyone gazed back at him earnest and eager, so he carried on. "They're dickheads, pseudo-revolutionaries. They're not about to kill anyone."

"So, it's likely that it was someone from the allotments," Lüdi concluded. "Perhaps someone closely connected to Flückiger. Füglistaller for example. It's possible that around 2 a.m., when everyone was drunk, he went to Flückiger's cabin. Flückiger was sitting at the table, already in his nightwear, with a bottle of wine and the gun in front of him. The visitor sits down and they share a glass of wine. They quarrel, they stagger around in the cabin, knocking over the bed and the chair. Then the visitor grabs the gun and shoots Flückiger in the forehead. But in that case, who pissed against the rosebush?"

"If it was Füglistaller, he may have been in his nightwear too," said Madörin. "He had gone to bed, but couldn't get to sleep. He thought about his dead rabbits, went across to Flückiger and shot him. Then he went outside into the snowy night and relieved himself by the rose bush. He saw the hooks hanging from his cabin next door."

"How could he see them, in the middle of the night?" asked Lüdi.

"He'd left the light on in his cabin. He fetched a hook, dragged the body outside and rammed the hook in under the chin. He tried to hang the body from the beam. As the beam was too high, he fetched a chair from inside the cabin and climbed onto it holding the corpse. When he was done, he put the chair back in the cabin."

"*Pourquoi pas?* Why not?" commented Madame Godet. "We found marks on the patio consistent with those left by chair legs."

"What about Stebler?" asked Lüdi. "Could he have helped him? And wouldn't their clothes have been covered in blood?"

"They could have changed their clothes, taken them home the following morning and got rid of them," said Madörin.

Everyone fell silent and pondered the possibilities. Yes, that's how it could have been, so simple and so brutal.

"And that's why, Madame, Messieurs, I would like to keep the gentlemen in until one of them tells the truth," Madörin concluded.

"What about the traces of Viagra found in Flückiger's blood?" Hunkeler commented.

"How do you mean?" Madörin asked, looking unsure.

"Could it have been a woman who visited Flückiger? Perhaps earlier in the evening, say at eight. She could have left him the Viagra and promised to come back at two. And when she came back, she shot him."

"And who would have hung him from the beam?" Madörin argued.

"Are you saying a woman could have done that?"

"It could have also been a man who gave him the Viagra," said Lüdi. "To get revenge."

"Disgusting," muttered Hunkeler and stood up. "Madame, Messieurs, I'll be in my office. If Bardet turns up, ask him to come and see me please."

As he left, he glimpsed Madörin looking at him venomously.

Hunkeler went into his office and closed the door, carefully and quietly, as if someone might be following him. He sat down on the chair, tipped it backwards and braced his feet against the desk. He stayed like that for a while, until he felt himself getting restless. He reached for his phone to call Hedwig, but decided against it. He didn't want to get on her nerves.

Then he realized how full of sorrow he felt. All day he hadn't noticed, he'd always been busy talking and listening. The encounters of the past days were weighing on him. The farmer's wife who had told him about the Ballersdorf lads when they were standing in the cowshed the previous evening. Then Frau Scholler in Knoeringue. This morning the mayor in Ballersdorf. The silent visitor at the cemetery.

Margot in the bookshop, who'd mentioned her husband's frozen feet. Old Rinser and his peculiar great-nephew. All of them had spoken of the horrors of the war. That horror was still in him now, he could feel it. He would have liked to cry, but that wasn't an option in the office.

He wondered why he'd found the briefing so tedious. It was perfectly normal for the crew to ponder the possible progression of events leading to the crime, though the ideas voiced today had been dull and vague. Often at such meetings, they came up with the most outlandish scenarios. Sometimes this was precisely what set them on the right path. And it couldn't be ruled out that someone like Füglistaller had picked up the gun. Even though this would be tantamount to an insult. An insult to Mara, to Sonja, to the silent visitor.

He stood up, took the sleeping mat out of the cupboard, unrolled it and laid down. He fell asleep immediately.

It was as if he was lying in his grave, stretched out straight and dead. He could still hear himself breathe, but he wasn't alive any more. He heard a knocking from above, from the earth's surface. It penetrated down to him and he knew he urgently needed to get up there, out of the darkness. He had to scratch and scrabble, force his way up, call out. But no sound came out of his mouth. He was enveloped by arms that were draped across his body, threatening to strangle him. Suddenly, he realized he was lying under the yew, that the tree's roots were growing around him and holding him down.

He opened his eyes. He struggled to get his bearings. In front of him stood Bardet, eyeing him warily.

"Are you not well? *Vous êtes malade?*"

Hunkeler sat up. Ah yes, he'd fallen asleep in his office. "No. Why?"

"You called out in your sleep. I couldn't understand a word. Do you need a doctor?"

"Not at all. I was just tired." He got up and put the mat away. Then he went over to the sink and splashed water on his face. "I was sad. *Triste*. Sleep heals everything, doesn't it?"

Bardet shook his head irritably. "You're a strange fellow."

"You've told me that already. Shall we go and eat?"

"*D'accord*," Bardet agreed, now grinning.

They crossed the Heuwaage viaduct and turned off into the Steinenvorstadt quarter. The snow here had been cleared away. Young revellers sat at the tables, shouting and drinking from beer bottles.

"Let's go to Adriano's," Hunkeler suggested. "I can get a pot of tea there."

"So you are ill after all."

"No. But I've got a belly full of boiled beef. From lunch."

They crossed Barfüsserplatz. Hunkeler looked up at the church to check whether the cross at the top of the gable was still slightly offset to the left. It was, which he found reassuring.

They sat down at a window table. Adriano came over to take their order.

"A pot of tea with cold milk," Hunkeler replied. "And do you have any black olives and sheep's cheese?"

"Yes. Today's special is veal shank with polenta."

"I'll have that," said Bardet. "And a good bottle of wine."

They both looked out onto the street, where people were passing by, staring in. Then they looked around the restaurant and at the mainly young clientele. Three old drunks were sitting at the table by the bar, Hunkeler knew them from the old days. "I used to go around boozing with those fellows over there," he said. "It was fun. Unfortunately it doesn't agree with me any more."

Bardet took a slug of wine. It was a Römerblut Pinot Noir from Valais. He seemed to be enjoying it.

The olives came and Hunkeler reached for some and chewed them slowly. He spat the stones into his left hand, then drank a cup of tea and poured himself some more.

"I know you had lunch in Knoeringue today," said Bardet. "And I also know who with. I know you were in Ballersdorf before that. I know who you talked to there. And I know that none of that was appropriate."

Hunkeler popped a piece of sheep's cheese into his mouth, then a bit of crusty white bread. "I have a house in Alsace, as you know. I can eat lunch wherever I want."

"True. But you're not allowed to make enquiries."

"Nonsense. I can talk to who I want."

Bardet hesitated, then sliced off a piece of the veal shank. "*Merveilleux*," he sighed.

Hunkeler ground some black pepper over the cheese. "Superb."

"How did you find out about it?" Bardet asked.

"From my neighbour. She'd read about Toni Flückiger's death, in the *Alsace*. It made her think of the lads from Ballersdorf. Of the story that is told about it. She said she wasn't sure whether it had happened the way people said it had. But she still told me. It seems the story is stronger than reality."

"I heard about it from my mother, she got me onto it. It's odd, really. I'm a born-and-bred Alsatian, I grew up and

207

went to school here. Yet I knew nothing about Ballersdorf."
He topped up his wine. "Will you have a glass with me?"

"Later, when I've finished my tea."

"Whether that's how it happened or not, the parallels are certainly striking," Bardet continued. Perhaps myth is always more powerful than reality. What do you think?"

"Yes, I agree. Monsieur Rinser's great-nephew, you might want to check him out sometime. He says it's not made up. He insisted that it happened the way people say it did. He's thinking of revenge. His name is Claude Schwob and he works at the Crédit Mutuel in Jettingen."

"I know," Bardet replied and pushed his empty plate aside. "We arrested him at his place of work at three this afternoon."

Hunkeler didn't speak for some time. It was back again, the feeling of sorrow, it was rising in his throat. "Right, let's get another bottle," he said. "I'll join you."

They ordered a second bottle and drank to each other's health. Then they looked out onto the street again. There was more snow again, falling in large, white flakes.

"It never ends," said Hunkeler. "One horror gives birth to the next."

"Oh, it will end. We'll make sure of that. It's time to stop with this nonsense."

"How did he track down Anton Russius?"

"He's a hacker. He's already been arrested once, but they had to let him go. He has friends, there's a whole group of them. They have a list of former Gestapo and SS people who were in Ballersdorf at the time. All old men now, of course. Some of the people on that list died in the tsunami in Thailand at the end of 2004. The old comrades. It seems they planned to murder all these men. Which I can understand in a way. Cigarette?"

Hunkeler helped himself to one of Bardet's black cigarettes.

"Claude Schwob is related to two men who were shot back in February 1943," Bardet continued. "He wanted to revenge the death of those men. In the early hours of New Year's Day, he and a friend drove to Hegenheim. They parked near the allotments. At half past two they entered the grounds and headed for B35. They had a gun and a meathook with them, and even a rope. They admitted all of this straight away. But they are adamant that they arrived too late. They say Russius was already hanging from the beam, with his forehead blown apart."

"How did you find Claude Schwob?"

"One of our border guards was on patrol round there on New Year's Eve. He saw the parked car. It struck him as suspicious, so he noted down the number."

"Why did you wait until this afternoon to arrest him?"

"We've been watching him since New Year's Day. We investigated his connections. The plan was to collar the entire group, and we've achieved that."

"It's difficult for me to collaborate in an investigation I'm not leading," commented Hunkeler. "I'm not used to it."

"You didn't tell me everything either. At least not straight away, *n'est-ce pas?*"

Hunkeler nodded, even though he felt he'd been taken for a ride. "Do you believe him?" he asked.

"I'm not sure. They're a strange bunch of lads. Actually, there are also two girls in the group. They say they want to defend Alsace. Against the east and the west. They say Alsace is an autonomous country, with its own language and culture."

"Well, they're right there."

"I think it's a load of nonsense. Alsace is part of France, *et fini.*"

"I'm assuming they accept that."

"Not entirely. They want some kind of federal independence, like the Swiss cantons have. That's how they describe it. By the way, it's important that we keep this under wraps. You're the only one at Basel CID I'm telling this. The press mustn't find out about it. *D'accord?*"

"My lips are sealed. But there are some crafty journalists out there. If Claude Schwob can find the former SS man Russius, then a large newspaper should be able to do it too."

"I don't think so. Claude Schwob is a real whizz-kid. He could easily have a stellar career in the IT sector. But he doesn't want that. He wants to serve Alsace, he said."

"An idealist then, so probably telling the truth. What are you going to do with them now?"

"All we can do is wait."

"He was wearing sports shoes at lunch today. It struck me as odd, with all this snow."

"Perhaps it's true," commented Bardet. "Perhaps they really were too late. Who knows?"

Around eleven, Hunkeler's phone rang. He didn't want to answer at first, but then he did anyway. It was Cattaneo.

"Listen to me, Hunkeler. I'm in my cabin on C25. I'm returning to the dead, where I came from. To Lucia. I want to be united with her, forever. Do you understand what I'm saying?"

"Just a moment," said Hunkeler and pressed the record button. "What are you talking about?"

"*Moment* is a stupid word. I'm departing this life, do you follow? I don't want to live any more. Even breathing is a burden, all this in and out. It's ridiculous. What for? Are you listening?"

"Yes, I'm listening. Just a second." He covered the mouthpiece. "It's Cattaneo. He's in his cabin."

Bardet was instantly alert. He pushed his glass aside. "Can I listen in?"

Hunkeler pressed the loudspeaker key. "What are you intending to do?" he asked.

"I'm going to hang myself. Just like I hanged Flückiger. Only without the gun or the hook. Just with a rope. The rope separates life from death."

Hunkeler waved Adriano over. "Quick, an ambulance, to the Stadtgärten-West allotments at Bachgraben. Tell them to send a French ambulance too. Not here at the table. Do it at the bar."

Adriano went back to the bar to make the call.

"Are you still there?" Cattaneo asked.

"Yes, of course I am. I'm always there for you."

"Forget the word *always*. There's no always in life, always exists only in death. Come over, untie me and close my eyes. The entrance is blocked. Take my way in. I walked through the Jewish cemetery and climbed over the fence. You'll see my tracks, follow them."

"Call the guard at the allotment entrance," Hunkeler instructed Bardet. "Tell him to run to C25, right now. I'll try to keep him talking."

"Was it really him?"

"Of course. You heard what he said."

"Who are you talking to?" Cattaneo asked. "Your girlfriend?"

"Yes. We're sitting in the living room. We've had a nice dinner. Now we're just chatting. Why don't you come over and have a drink with us?"

"No, I've had plenty of drinks. Eventually every glass is empty. I want to drink from Lethe, the river of forgetfulness. I committed murder, I killed my wife's lover. Instead of protecting him, I killed him. First my wife, then her lover. What do you think of that?"

"Just a minute. Don't hang up."

Outside, he saw Bardet running down the street through dense flurries of snow. He saw him stopping a taxi and racing away in it.

"Right," he said. "I've sorted myself out now. I can chat now. Isn't it a bit cold in the cabin, with all this snow coming down?"

"No, the snow is good. It covers everything, and everything is pure. Who's that talking in the background? I can hear voices."

"It's the television. I can switch it off if it's annoying you."

"Yes, it's annoying. Very annoying. This is a sacred hour. The hour of transition. We will be a trio, a triad, merry and joyful. Lucia, Toni and Ettore. He can sleep with her, of course he can. Any time. I didn't kill him out of jealousy, I killed him out of desperation. And loneliness. There's no loneliness in death. Do you follow me, Hunkeler? I have these thoughts, I could shift the earth out of its orbit with these thoughts. But nobody will listen to me."

"I'm listening to you. Do you know what? Why don't I come over to you. I'll bring a good bottle of wine. Turn the heater up, so we'll be nice and warm."

"No, I'm not going back in the cabin. I'm standing on a chair, the rope is around my neck. One step and I'm dead."

Hunkeler gripped his wine glass. He became aware of the complete silence that had spread across the room. Adriano stood in front of him, he wanted to help. "Go away," Hunkeler whispered. "You're disturbing me."

Adriano took three steps back.

"Cheers," said Hunkeler and drank. He noticed his hand was wet with sweat. "See, I've switched off the television now."

"Yes. It's quiet now. Deathly quiet."

"No," Hunkeler shouted. "What are you doing? You don't need to speed up death. It will arrive of its own accord when the time comes."

"Finally you've understood. I want to dictate the passing of time. I can't bear this damned waiting around." Cattaneo was crying, Hunkeler could hear it clearly.

"You've already taken the step that separates life from death," said Hunkeler. "You committed the crime. You set Toni Flückiger free."

The sobbing stopped. "How do you mean?"

"Of course you did. You freed him from life."

There was a long pause. "It wasn't that easy," Cattaneo finally said. "I had a knife on me when I went to see him. But I'm not sure whether I would have had the courage to push it into his body. Then I saw his gun lying on the table, a Swiss army gun. That's when I knew I would do it. We drank some wine. I called him to account over Lucia. He said a woman was allowed to decide for herself who she wanted to sleep with. He said he'd been stood up himself that evening, even though he was well prepared. Then he realized the danger and tried to flee. I shot him in the forehead. He stumbled over the bed, but he was dead. Are you following me, Hunkeler?"

"Yes, of course. Carry on, I'm listening, I have time."

A distant siren could be heard in the background.

"What's that?" Cattaneo asked.

"I can hear a siren. It seems to be some way off. Probably an accident somewhere."

"I dragged him outside, I don't know why. Then I saw the meathooks hanging on Füglistaller's cabin. I fetched one and pushed it in under his chin. There was a rope hanging from the roof beam. I tied it to the hook and tried to pull him up by it. I couldn't get him up. I got a chair from the cabin and climbed onto it with Toni in my arms. I was able to pull him up then. I didn't think I'd be able to do it at first. But then I managed. Surprising, isn't it?"

"Yes, very surprising."

A second siren could be heard. It seemed to be coming closer.

"I was covered in blood. It was revolting. I put on one of Toni's old coats and used the sleeve to wipe down everything I had touched. Then I went home. Giovanna cried when she saw me. She was afraid of me. I told her what I had done. She never said another word to me. Can you understand that, Hunkeler? Death is very close."

"Did you know his real name?"

214

"What real name?"

"He was a poor wretch, really."

"Yes. A wretched pig. Pigs are slaughtered and hung up. That's what they're there for. We're all wretched pigs. You too, Hunkeler. I could offer you an Armagnac. I've bought a bottle. Something to help us pass what's left of this evening, what do you think, Hunkeler?"

"Yes, let's knock a few back together. I'll be with you in a couple of minutes."

Another pause. The sirens were close now.

"What's going on? I can see a light coming towards me. I can hear steps. Have you betrayed me? Why? Goodbye, Hunkeler. *Addio*, farewell."

There was a faint crack. It was more of a crunch. Then silence. Steps. A man's voice came on.

"*Qui est là?* Who's there?"

"Hunkeler, Basel CID. Who are you?"

"*Merde*. What a mess." Then the connection was cut.

Hunkeler sat there on his chair, the dead phone in his hand. He could feel sweat running down his cheeks in ice-cold drops. The phone slipped from his hand and fell onto the floor.

Complete silence still enveloped the room. Everyone was looking at the old man sitting at his table, exhausted, white as a sheet.

Adriano picked up the phone. "Is he dead?"

Hunkeler nodded slowly. "There was a crunching sound," he said.

"Did he hang himself? Or how…"

Hunkeler looked up. He saw the timeless face of an old man, the little purple veins, the dark rings under the eyes, the inquisitive, sympathetic expression. "He has said goodbye to life. Goodbyes are always sad," Hunkeler replied.

Adriano nodded and went to the bar without taking his eyes off Hunkeler. He pushed down the lever of the espresso machine. There was a quiet hissing, familiar and wonderfully ordinary.

He brought the cup to the table and Hunkeler drank. "Thank you, my friend," he said.

"You're welcome. I think if someone is determined to do it, one should let them go."

"Don't, please. Can I pay?"

"Not necessary. You can pay next time, if you want."

People had started talking again. Orders were being placed. A glass of wine, a beer, a coffee. Hunkeler pulled out his handkerchief and wiped his face. Then he left.

There were only a few people left on the street, it was snowing too heavily. It was a warm, wet snow. It wouldn't stay on the ground for long.

Hunkeler got a taxi. They headed north, towards the border. A number 3 tram was trundling along in front of them, the driver couldn't overtake. "*Che maledetto*," he swore. Hunkeler didn't care. He had all the time in the world.

He saw the towers of the Spalentor glide past, barely recognizable in the driving snow. Then Burgfelderplatz and Kannenfeld Park, where Erkan's cafe was wrapped in darkness.

At the Luzernerring, the lights were still on. Then came the road to Hegenheim, and the entrance to the allotments.

A Basel ambulance was parked outside. The medic, a young wiry fellow, stood leaning against the rear door, smoking. Prosecutor Suter was already there, with a large red umbrella. Next to him stood Lüdi, Haller, Madörin and contact man Morath.

"I don't know how he got in," said Haller.

"Probably through the Jewish cemetery. We can't cover everything."

Madörin stood there with a hangdog expression, looking embarrassed. He'd been off the mark again, like everyone else. "At least it was one of the allotment holders," he said bitterly. "And I couldn't arrest them all."

"Don't worry," Hunkeler replied. "We were all wrong."

"Was it definitely him?" asked Suter. "Can you testify to that? Am I free to inform the press accordingly?"

"Ask Bardet. He listened in."

"Why couldn't you prevent him from taking his life?"

Hunkeler's eyes narrowed, he only just managed to stop himself from throwing a punch.

Prosecutor Suter took a step back and put his left hand to his throat. "Sorry, I didn't mean it like that," he said.

"How then?" Hunkeler growled.

He walked away from the group and took a few steps into the allotments. The glare of floodlights cut through the low trees again, softened by the falling snow. He heard the Hegenheim church clock strike, it was half past twelve.

Eventually he heard a vehicle approaching from C25. Two headlights appeared and quickly grew larger. It was the French ambulance, taking away Ettore Cattaneo's body. The group watched the vehicle pass, wordlessly, without moving. The Swiss medic flicked his cigarette into the snow in a wide arc, got in and drove off towards Basel.

"That's it then," said Suter. "The case has been solved." He wasn't sure whether to appear sorrowful or happy. He opted for sober gravity. "It's regrettable that there had to be a further victim. But when someone wants to go, they should be allowed to. The press conference will take place at eleven tomorrow. I'm expecting you all to be there."

"Sorry, I can't come," replied Hunkeler.

"What? You have to come, you were the last person to talk to the offender."

"I'm too tired, too spent. Believe me, I would only cry."

"A crying inspector? Whatever next? How do you think that would look?"

Hunkeler reached into his pocket and pulled out his phone. "Here, take this. The conversation was recorded, apart from the first few sentences. It's all on there, how he killed Flückiger, his motives. And why he wanted to die. And I'm sure Bardet will be there, he can confirm everything."

Suter took the phone and slipped it into his pocket. "You are the most impossible man I've ever come across," he grumbled. He got in his car and drove off.

The rest of them went to get a coffee in the Blume, which was open. News of Cattaneo's death had got round, the regulars' table was full.

"Will our friends be released now?" asked Siegrist.

"I'm sure they will," Hunkeler replied. "It's clear they had nothing to do with the murder."

Hunkeler and his colleagues wordlessly drank their coffee. A weary, exhausted, useless troop.

At 1 a.m. Hauser came in. He was in a great rush. He sat down next to Hunkeler. "Do you know what the tabloid will be saying tomorrow?" he asked.

"I have no idea."

"That Toni Flückiger was actually called Russius. That he was in the SS and took part in the massacre of young lads in Ballersdorf near Altkirch in February 1943. That there's a young Alsatian group that wants to avenge this massacre. And that this group broke into the allotments on New Year's Eve, where they shot Russius and hung him up."

"Fascinating," Hunkeler replied, "but not true."

"I heard that the perpetrator is an allotment holder and that he hanged himself this evening on his allotment."

Hunkeler was instantly wide awake again. "Where did you hear that? From Adriano?"

"You know I never reveal my sources."

Hunkeler drank the rest of his coffee, very slowly, even though it had gone cold. "When's your deadline?" he asked.

"That's long passed."

"Good. The press conference is tomorrow at eleven. They will then announce what everyone in this room already knows."

"Which is?"

"Ask the regulars here. They'll happily tell you. The perpetrator hanged himself about an hour and a half ago. The stuff about the Alsatian group is rubbish."

Hunkeler slept in his Basel apartment that night, right through to ten o'clock in the morning. Sergeant Kaelin had driven him home at half past two. He'd opened the balcony door. The snow had given way to rain and as he'd listened, he'd fallen into a deep, dreamless sleep.

He walked into the Sommereck at half past eleven.

"Here, have a read of what it says in the tabloid," Edi greeted him.

"No thanks, I'm not interested," Hunkeler replied.

"What? An Alsatian gang breaks into Basel's community allotments and murders a man, and you're not interested?"

"No. It's all a pack of lies. Listen to Radio Basilisk at twelve. Then you'll hear the truth."

"My God, what kind of world do we live in? Who can you still trust these days? By the way, I happened to come into possession of a *saucisson vaudois*. Home-made by a farmer up in the Jura Mountains. That's the genuine article, you can definitely trust that. An absolute delight with mustard and fresh rolls."

"Dish it up then, let's dig in."

He only ate a few slices. The rest disappeared into Edi's paunch. Hunkeler slowly drank two cups of milky coffee, relishing them. He didn't read any of the papers, he wasn't in the mood.

He watched the guests as they came in, ordered and drank. A young couple sipping cola and holding hands. A lonely pensioner who leafed through the *Basler Zeitung* for nearly an hour. Three old women, all dressed up for the weekend. It was a peaceful Saturday morning. The workers had finished for the week. And old inspectors were also looking forward to their two days off.

Around twelve he set off into town. In the Spalenberg quarter he went into a bookshop and asked for a book about Colmar. They didn't have any, so he looked at the recent literary publications. In the end he bought an older book, a biography of Albert Camus. He was looking forward to it. To Oran, to the Maghreb, to the existentialist period in Paris.

He carried on across Barfüsserplatz and through the Steinenvorstadt quarter. The rain was pelting down. It was a proper, steady downpour that washed away the snow. By the Heuwaage viaduct he entered the high-rise and took the elevator up to Harry's sauna. Three rounds of sweating as always, and cold water in between. Then he took the stairs up to the roof terrace and let the rain patter down on him.

At four he set off to Colmar. He drove onto the motorway and put his foot down, with the window wide open. The rain was streaming in, but he didn't care. "I love Paris in the springtime," he sang at the top of his voice. "I love Paris in the fall." He sang it first in minor, then in major. He repeated this several times, until he got tired of it. He fiddled with the car radio, looking for some music he liked. There was a programme on Teddy Wilson, elegant and swinging. He was reminded then that Swing had been his nickname at college. It made him grin.

He parked by Colmar's city wall and looked for the Hotel Le Maréchal. It was on the banks of the Lauch river, a luxury hotel. That suited him very well. He told the staff on the reception desk that his girlfriend was expecting him. They handed him the keys and he went upstairs. The room looked out over the water. He laid down on the bed and tried to immerse himself in Camus's childhood. He nodded off a few pages in and didn't wake up until Hedwig walked in.

He pretended to be asleep and waited for her to sit down beside him on the bed.

"Finally," she whispered. "Have you got time now?"

Without a word, he locked her into his arms.

"Not so fast," she said. "Wait until I'm undressed."

The following morning at ten, they strolled through the old town centre to the Dominican Church. Mass had just finished and a throng of people was emerging, dressed in their Sunday best. The sound of a church organ could be heard from inside.

They went in and sat down on a pew in front of the *Madonna of the Rose Garden*, painted by Martin Schongauer in 1473. It showed a young, gentle, pensive woman with her naked child on her arm, surrounded by roses that seemed to have grown especially for her. Two angels held a heavenly crown above her. There were birds too. Sparrows, chaffinches, robins, great tits. Two goldfinches perched among the roses to the right, and the ground was dotted with ripe strawberries.

"Just like our garden," said Hedwig. "Except that we don't have any roses."

"Yes. Perhaps we should plant a rose hedge."

"No," she decided. "The garden is fine how it is. We even have bats."

"True. There aren't any bats on here."

"Because it's daytime, you nitwit. They only come out at dusk."

Hunkeler carefully studied the woman's red gown. Her pale brown hair spilling down over it. Her long, delicate fingers, the toes of the child. "Do you know how to cross yourself?" he asked.

"Why would I? I'm not Catholic."

"Try it."

Hedwig tried, but didn't know how.

"I wonder what the Madonna makes of your antics," he commented.

"She likes to have a laugh too."